THE CAR

THE CAR
MITCHELL HADLEY

THROCKMORTON PRESS
MINNEAPOLIS, MINNESOTA

Author photo by J.A. McKinney

First Printing, 2016

ISBN: 978-1-7326207-1-1
ISBN-10: 1732620717

Throckmorton Press LLC
2551 38th Avenue NE, #335
Minneapolis, MN 55421

If you want a happy ending, that depends, of course, on where you stop your story.

- Orson Welles

CHAPTER 1

It begins with the car.

There is nothing remarkable about it. It has four tires, two doors, a steering wheel and an engine. License plates on the front and back bumpers, and a roomy trunk. It is like any other car you might see parked on a city street. A blue car, perhaps. Yes, let's just go ahead and call it blue. As for the make and model, that too is open to conjecture. Groucho advertises for DeSoto, and with the Red Scare in the daily headlines, you could hardly get more topical than Marx. And his program, You Bet Your Life, has a most appropriate title, as you will see. But it is a fact that few readers today will recall the DeSoto, let alone Groucho, and so it would be better to imagine a more contemporary brand. The Thunderbird was brand new that year, but a little too ostentatious. Chevy, perhaps? After all, you can see the U.S.A. in your Chevrolet, according to Dinah Shore.

Yes, that will do—a blue Chevy Bel Air, with sleek chrome stylings and the rocket-shaped hood ornament that points the way toward a future of limitless possibilities.

Upon further examination, however, you may notice one thing about the car that does differentiate it from the others parked along the street this afternoon. Looking at the front windshield, you can't help but notice a number of slips of paper slapped on it—there, stuck underneath the wiper blades, the red stripe across the bottom identifying them as parking tickets. And to judge by the number of them attached to the car, it has been going on for some time. Today you might see a boot clamped on one of the tires, but then our story begins before the time of conveniences such as a boot.

Perhaps someone forgot to refill the meter. Perhaps the car is parked too near a fire hydrant. Perhaps the car is in a no-parking zone, identified by the yellow painted stripe along the curb, which may have been worn away by time and the elements. There are many possibilities, but none of them are particularly important to us right now. What is certain is that every day or two, a new ticket appears underneath the wiper, and every day the car remains parked in the same place.

Why the blue Chevy remains there collecting tickets is a mystery. A friend in the police department told me that it wasn't their job to analyze these things. We only look at the facts. If a car is parked somewhere it shouldn't be, we give it a ticket and notify the towing company. If the car hasn't moved, it's them you should be talking to.

The man at the towing company offered a different story when I asked him about it. We only do what we're told to do, he said. We get an order to pick up a car, one of my drivers is there within two hours. Our business depends on speed–that's how we make our money. If we don't tow the cars when we're supposed to, nobody else gets to park there, and we don't get any new business.

Whatever the reason, there is no denying that anyone who walks this way on a regular basis would be bound to notice the blue car with its continuing accumulation of tickets on the front windshield, and that other than a new ticket every couple of days, everything else remained the same.

And so this is where it begins. It begins now, it begins before the womb, before conception.

This is where it begins.

◆ ◆ ◆

It begins with Winter.

Like the car, there is nothing particularly noteworthy about Winter. We know, for example, that he was the third of four children, with two sisters and an older brother. We know that when he was young he had a dog named Bosco, and he used to play sandlot baseball, back when kids did things like that. His friends called him Sandy, because of his red hair, and he burns easily if he's in the sun without a hat. He probably would have fought in the recent war if he hadn't been classified as 4F due to flat feet. We know these things, and a great deal more, but none of it is particularly important to us right now.

Today Winter is an average man, around thirty, with an average job—an insurance company, perhaps? Yes: he is a claims adjustor with an insurance company, one of the pillars of post-war American business. As such, he spends a great deal of time going in and out of the office in one of the company cars, and when he is in the office it is a steel gray cubicle surrounded by other steel gray cubicles, with a couple of filing cabinets nearby and a typewriter to one side on a small table. While claims work isn't the most exciting in the world, it provides steady work, and Winter is good at it. Plus, there are management possibilities down the road. Truth be told, however, there are times when it becomes easy for Winter to go on automatic pilot and still get the job done.

At roughly the same time each day, he stacks his papers neatly on his desk, pushes back his chair, puts on his fedora and goes to the automat across the street for lunch. Generally he shares the lunch counter with one of three people: a doctor from the building a block away, an accountant from the building next door, a lawyer from the floor downstairs. The doctor tells him about his latest patient, the accountant about the problems one of his clients has, the lawyer about his latest case. None of them know Winter well enough to call him Sandy. Most of the time Winter listens, nods, adds some questions of his own. Rarely does he interject anything about his own job. There are particular meals that he favors, but to suggest that he eats the same thing each day would be going too far. He is not a dull man, but neither does he go out of his way to cultivate adventure.

At the end of the day Winter duplicates the procedure he follows at lunch and leaves the building, but instead of heading right (toward the automat), he goes to the left where he catches a bus for home. It's not that he doesn't own a car of his own, but it is much easier to take the bus downtown than it is to try and find a place to park. After about ten minutes, he disembarks from the bus and walks a block to his apartment, a third-floor walkup among a group of brownstones in a gently aging neighborhood. Often in the evening he goes out with friends, or walks down to the bar a couple of blocks to the west, where he might have a couple of beers while talking with the bartender or a couple of the regulars. The conversation is much the same as it is at lunch, except here Winter is more animated, as the discussion turns to baseball or football (depending on the season), politics, or something else that has appeared in the headlines.

On the nights when he does not go out he fixes his dinner in a small efficiency kitchen, or picks up something on the way home. He eats at a small table just outside the kitchen, watches the new television set he bought last year with the year-end bonus (a 12-inch RCA, which means he doesn't always have to head down to the bar for entertainment), listens to some music on the radio, or reads. Some evenings he masturbates thinking about the vice president's secretary, with whom he will soon have a brief fling that, while enjoyable, yields somewhat less than was promised by the fantasies he engages in late at night. In his dreams he imagines she is calling him Sandy.

◆ ◆ ◆

It's normal for someone to notice a ticketed car; there's often a feeling of empathy that goes through the system, thinking of the reaction the car's owner will have when he comes out of wherever he happens to be and discovers the ticket. It may be someone who is mildly irritated by the expense that the ticket will mean, or it may be that something will not be purchased, some act not consummated, as a result of the loss of money that accompanies the ticket. Sometimes it's a gamble gone wrong, a roll of the dice that the driver will be able to get away before the cops notice; mostly, it's a result of poor planning, or an errand taking longer than originally thought. It's hard not to feel sorry for someone in this situation though, don't you think?

This is what Winter tells himself as he sits at his desk on this particular afternoon. He makes the motions of going through the file on his latest claim, but his mind is distracted by something that has nothing to do with his work, something that doesn't really concern him personally at all, unless he were to choose to make it his business, and there's no reason why he should do that. It is a ridiculous thing that has distracted him, Winter thinks, bordering on stupidity, and he can justify it only by blaming a bored mind, but the distraction exists nonetheless. It has to do with a blue car that he has seen parked across the street from his office, not far from the automat where he goes for lunch. As a matter of fact, he first saw the car last week while heading to meet the doctor, whose name is Richards, at the automat.

No, he thinks, that's not quite right. Though it is perhaps the first time he has noticed it, paid any attention to it, it could not have been the first time he has actually seen the car. For if this was the case, then he would not have remarked on the parking tickets gracing the front windshield. This happened on the day he met Collins in the lobby, from which the two of them would head to the automat for lunch.

As they leave the building that noon, Collins asks Winter if they can make a quick detour to the bank, about a block away, so that Collins can deposit a check he's received from a client. I want to get it in the bank before it has a chance to bounce, he says with a wry amusement that doesn't conceal a particular truth about some of Collins' clients.

Leaving the bank, on the way to the automat, they pass the blue car.

Will you look at that? Winter says to Collins.

Look at what? Collins replies.

The car, Winter says.

What about it?

Just look at the tickets on the windshield.

Yeah, sorry bastard. He'll be out a few bucks when he gets done paying that.

That's not it. I mean, look at all those tickets.

Which is why it's going to cost him.

But this car must have been parked here for a while.

That, Collins says with a mild amusement, would be a reasonable conclusion.

So why hasn't the car been towed away?

You tell me. I'm a lawyer, not a policeman.

And why would someone just leave a car like that here? You'd think he'd miss it by now.

I'm not a mind reader either, Collins replies.

The conversation is cut off as the two men enter the automat, where they join Driscoll, the accountant, and Richards, the doctor, and soon it is all but forgotten about, what with a ham sandwich and potato chips to concentrate on. As to whether or not the car is still there when the men leave to return to work, you could not prove it by Winter, whose mind has already moved to the files that taunt him on his desk, demanding his attention.

In fact, I suspect the car would have disappeared completely from Winter's consciousness had it not been for an unplanned trip to see Richards, the doctor, later that week. Richards is not his regular doctor, but Winter has been suffering from a rash on the back of his hand for the past couple of days, and when he mentioned it to Richards at lunch yesterday the doctor had said he'd be glad to take a look at it the next day.

After receiving a prescription for a topical cream that Winter should apply on the rash (twice daily for a week; if you don't see any improvement by then, call me), Winter headed back to the office, taking the opposite side of the street from that which he'd walked on when he'd headed to see Richards. And it is there that he once more sees the car.

Except for another ticket or two on the windshield, the car looks to be exactly the same as it was the previous time Winter saw it. This time, without an empty stomach bearing down on him, he pauses to study the vehicle a little more closely. To be sure, it is not this year's model, but is at least a couple of years old. For that, though, it seems to be in very good condition, with no obvious signs of rust, nor any chrome hanging off from the fenders, front or rear of the car. The sunlight reflects off its shiny blue surface, and if the car has not been washed recently, Winter would say it hasn't been left in the open for very long, either. From what he can tell, the interior of the car appears to be in equally good shape.

Which once again begs the question, the one which Winter had started to ask when he and Collins had discussed it: why would anyone just abandon a perfectly good vehicle? And why would they do so in a location virtually guaranteed to draw a ticket from a traffic cop? Winter truly is surprised that the car hasn't already been towed away, something for which the owner—whoever it is—can be grateful. If, that is, he doesn't waste time retrieving the car, before it's too late.

Later, sitting at his desk in the office, Winter continues to puzzle over the car. A claims adjuster, like anyone who makes a living working with figures, likes to have everything balance out when it reaches the bottom line. Something like this just doesn't make sense, and if there's one thing Winter has learned over the years, it's that when something just doesn't make sense, there's usually a reason behind it. Perhaps if his day had been busier, if there had been a crisis clamoring for his attention, he wouldn't have had so much time to think about it, and the things to come might have turned out differently, but there is no percentage to be gained from retrospective thought.

This is where it begins.

CHAPTER 2

*A*bove the bar Pete has the TV on to Pabst Blue Ribbon
Bouts, with Russ Hodges calling the action, an indif-
ferent contest between a pair of featherweights, live
from Detroit. From time to time Winter hears the
shouts of the crowd as one or another of the fight-
ers lands a punch, but with Driscoll's commentary
going on he finds it difficult to concentrate on the
action.

They're at The Ratskeller, a bar a few blocks
from where Winter lives, and every Wednesday
night Pete has the Blue Ribbon Bouts on. Winter
had agreed to meet Driscoll around eight or so,
when they'd have a couple of beers and some nuts
and watch the fight, the way they often do on
Wednesdays. The crowd in the bar tonight isn't as
large as it is for the big fights, and so if Winter were
paying attention to what Driscoll was saying, he'd
have a better chance of hearing him than when the

bar is packed, when the title's on the line.

He hears the bell ring, and Hodges saying There's the end of round seven, and then it's the Pabst jingle to the tune of Ten Little Indians: Fresher, Cleaner, Smoother flavor, Zest & sparkle millions favor, Get that fresher, smoother flavor, Pabst Blue Ribbon beer.

He's a slippery one, says Driscoll.

What?

Pep. Tough to hit. No wonder they call him The Will o' the Wisp.

If you say so. You're the expert, says Winter.

Ordinarily Winter welcomes Driscoll's company, at least as a diversion to the events of the day. Winter is usually content to let Driscoll carry the conversation since he is one of those people who has an opinion on everything, whether sports, politics or women. Driscoll will speak in a loud, confident voice when it comes to the first two subjects (louder and more confident when he has had more than a couple of beers), but when the discussion turns to women his voice will drop to a conspiratorial, just-you-and-me tone, as he shares his latest adventures with the fair sex. Just last week he was telling Winter about his rendezvous with a young woman named Shelly who works in the secretarial pool at the accounting firm. Winter suspects that half of what Driscoll tells him is bluster, but there is enough truth in what he says to get Winter's interest up. You know what women are like, Driscoll says with a knowing wink, and Winter agrees.

Tonight, however, Winter has been distracted for most of the evening–even Driscoll's story of what he and Shelly were up to while her roommate was out shopping does not particularly interest him–and now he's not quite sure why he agreed to get together tonight in the first place.

The bell rings for the start of round eight. Pete puts another couple of bottles of Pabst in front of them. Driscoll has moved on from the fight, and is now talking about Ike and the Cold War. He may have gotten us out of Korea, Driscoll says, but now we're right in the middle of another war.

At least we're not firing any shots, Winter says.

Not yet, Driscoll replies. But who knows how long that's going to continue? Should never have let Russia get The Bomb. Thank God he's got Nixon in there. At least there's someone in the administration who isn't afraid to stand up to the Reds. In case Eisenhower doesn't run next year.

Why, have you heard something the rest of us haven't? Winter asks.

Of course not. But don't be silly. Ike's not a young man any more. Who knows what he'll decide to do? And at that age you never know how your health is going to be. Better that we have someone waiting in the wings, in case something happens.

Winter mulls this over, and as Driscoll continues his analysis he is interrupted by a shout from some of the others sitting at the end of the bar. Winter looks up at the flickering black and white screen to see that the bout has ended, with Pep, whose real name is Guglielmo Papaleo, winning a convincing ten-round decision. The fight, Hodges is saying, was never in doubt.

Cadilli wasn't much of a match for him, Driscoll says, and Winter has no choice but to agree, since it would be difficult for him to offer any evidence to the contrary. Not only has he been distracted this evening, he has been this way for much of the day, for Winter has finally arranged for a date tomorrow night with the vice president's secretary, dinner and a movie, and his mind races, thinking about it all and wishing that it was 24 hours later than it actually is. Though he thought the fight, combined with Driscoll's company, would be enough to turn him around, he can now see that he was mistaken.

Winter cups a handful of nuts and takes a final swallow of the Pabst before setting the bottle down on the bar. Time to be shoving off, he says, I need to be in the office early tomorrow.

He says good night to Driscoll, tells Pete he will be seeing him around, and heads back down the street toward his apartment. Winter is not generally a heavy drinker, but the atmosphere inside the bar has made him a little woozy and he is glad for the chance to walk in the fresh air and clear his head.

It is an early summer evening and the windows are open in many of the brownstones that he walks by, allowing him to hear the sounds coming from the apartments, letting him learn more about the lives of the people who live behind those windows. Classical music from one, and he thinks they might be listening to the NBC Symphony on the radio. A man and woman arguing in another, with a child's cries cutting through their words. A young couple sits on the fire escape, enjoying the evening air while listening to a transistor radio playing Bill Haley. Winter thinks he can see the girl's mother hovering in the background, keeping an eye on the two. If he could filter it all out, reduce it to so much white noise, he would hear only the sounds of his footsteps, followed a split second later by the echo formed from the brownstones. It would sound almost as if he were being followed–when he walks, the echo follows closely behind; when he stops, the pursuing echo stops as well.

By the time he reaches his own apartment, it has grown dark enough that the lights from behind the windows have become visible, merging with the streetlamps to provide a yellowish illumination on the otherwise black landscape. Mounting the steps to the entrance, he takes a quick glance back to make sure there is, indeed, no one following him. If there is, there is no sign, no shining pair of eyes staring back at him.

In bed, he thinks about the mother keeping an eye on the girl and her boyfriend sitting on the fire escape. That night, he dreams that he has been followed home by someone driving the blue car, keeping their eyes on him all the way home.

CHAPTER **3**

And now it is Friday night, and Winter is at last on his date with the vice president's secretary, who is called Sharon. He picks her up at the apartment she shares with a girlfriend, and then they are off. The evening begins with dinner at a downtown restaurant which Winter can barely afford, it will mean beans and franks for a week, but it is essential in order to make the right impression on a woman who is used to being close to power and money, two things which Winter does not have in abundance. Despite having prepared himself, he is still shocked when he sees the prices on the menu, and a lump forms in his throat, which he covers by drinking a glass of water. Make that two weeks of beans and franks, he thinks to himself.

After dinner they walk to the Bijou for the movie that many people are talking about, The Seven Year Itch, starring Marilyn Monroe as a beautiful woman known simply as The Girl, and Tom Ewell as her downstairs neighbor Sherman, a married man who has become friendly with The Girl and falls for her. And who can blame him, after all, for Marilyn Monroe is America's Sweetheart, the woman every man is in love with, with the smoldering sex appeal that every woman wishes she had.

In the story, Sherman's wife and son have left New York City in order to vacation in Maine for the summer, leaving Sherman and his fantasies to run wild. He first imagines himself trying to explain to his absent wife how none of the things he imagines can be his fault; since he is so irresistible to women, these kinds of incidents are bound to happen. To his distress, he imagines his wife's reaction as neither understanding (which would be too much to ask for) nor outrage (meaning she cares for him and will fight to keep him), but laughter. He is stung by her response, even though it comes from his own mind and not his wife's words, which he has merely imagined.

And is the thought that he is a magnet for women really that far-fetched an idea? While he and The Girl play Chopsticks on the piano in his apartment, he fantasizes that he is instead playing a Rachmaninoff piano concerto, which causes her to become overcome with emotion. Caught up in the power of his own fantasy, he makes a pass at her, but they wind up falling off the piano bench.

After she has left, he becomes wracked with guilt—after all, fantasies are one thing, but trying to put them into practice is something else entirely), and imagines that The

Girl tells the plumber what Sherman has done, in the process comparing him to the monster from a popular horror movie of the time, The Creature from the Black Lagoon. As this scenario spirals out of control, he envisions the news spreading all over town, until it makes its way up to Maine, where his wife and son find out about it–encouraging her to embark on an affair of her own.

As if in retribution for her imaginary infidelity, he is encouraged to take The Girl to a movie–The Creature from the Black Lagoon, in fact. It is after Sherman and The Girl leave the movie, as they are walking home, that the iconic scene occurs where Marilyn Monroe stands on the subway grate and the wind blows her skirt in the wind. As they watch the scene, Winter feels Sharon's knee brush against his own. At first he thinks it is simply an accidental touch, but when she then begins to deliberately rub her knee up and down against Winter's leg, he knows that the conclusion to their evening has already been determined.

It is quite unlike the end to the movie, in which Sherman engages in a final daydream, that of his wife returning to New York City from Maine in order to shoot him for the way he has carried on while she has been gone. The shock of this fantasy causes Sherman to come to his senses, after which he leaves for Maine to join his family, and everyone lives happily ever after.

Leaving the theater, Winter hesitantly reaches to take Sharon's hand as they cross the street, concerned that he may have misread her actions, but he is encouraged when she does not let go of his hand after they have reached the other side. She suggests coming up to her apartment for a nightcap–since, she adds with a smile, her roommate is gone for the weekend. We can have some privacy–Sandy.

Later that night, Winter will lie awake in her bed, staring up through the darkness at the ceiling of the strange room, listening to the electric hum of the alarm clock, unable to quite yet get to sleep though Sharon sleeps soundly next to him. He has been left restless and unsatisfied by the evening and its denouement and a vague feeling of unease natters at him, a feeling which does not disappear until he has returned from a trip to the bathroom, where he not only takes a piss but also washes himself off (even though he will shower before leaving in the morning). Oh well, he thinks–you can't always dictate how things will go, especially when there's more than one person involved. Life is not a novel, and you are not the author.

As he finally drifts off to sleep he imagines himself standing on the corner, watching Sharon drive off in the blue car along with Tom Ewell and Marilyn Monroe, waving goodbye as they disappear around a bend.

CHAPTER 4

It is Monday, a day which has never been a favorite of Winter's but today it is even more disagreeable than usual. Oh, he's getting his work done all right, but such is the nature of his job that he can function efficiently while his mind is elsewhere, and today it is definitely not at the office.

For one thing, he is still suffering the aftereffects from his liaison with Sharon. There was nothing wrong with it, exactly, but that initial impression, lying in her bed in the night darkness, was one of isolation, of feeling completely alone, and that sense has only intensified in the day and a half since then. Perhaps it wasn't her fault, entirely, or even mostly; he received no complaints from her as he dressed to leave. He likens it to a meal that leaves a bad taste in the mouth afterward, and he has already determined to keep his distance from her, to have as little to do with her as possible from now on. Whatever happens after this will be without his encouragement.

Then, of course, there is the car. It was all he could do to keep from driving downtown on Sunday to check up on it, and now he thinks perhaps he should have, just in case someone drove the car during the weekend and returned it before the start of the day. He thinks it unlikely, however, particularly since his stroll over there this morning revealed yet another ticket stuck under the windshield wiper. What does that make now? Five? Six? He isn't sure, but it's enough to convince him that the car has been rooted to that place for some time.

After lunch (an egg salad sandwich, which he consumes while reviewing the games of the past weekend with Richards), he checks on it again, even though by now he takes it for granted it will be found in the same spot, as indeed it is. Now he finds his mind growing ever more distant from his work, and when he finds himself reading the same paragraph in the accident report for the fourth time, he knows he might as well just give up, so he shuts the file and places it back in the in-box on his desk. This in and of itself does not trouble him; he is known for his efficiency, and will have no trouble catching up.

In the meantime he has been aimlessly doodling on the yellow pad in front of him, the one with the green cover, and he now finds that he has drawn a succession of diagonal lines, slanting from right to left, and then has crossed through them with parallel lines. Forming–what? Crosses, yes, or lower-case letter ts, or the letter X, over and over.

Yes, he thinks, that's what he's been writing all along, unaware of his subconscious mind at work. X, the mystery letter, always used to signify the unknown. Dimension X, the old radio program, featuring adventures in time and space. The X-1 rocket plane, the one that Yeager used to break the sound barrier, the invisible impenetrable, unbreakable until it was broken. X-Rays, the unseen waves of radiation that shoot through the body and transmit their ghostly images against black transparencies. X marks the spot, the mystery location of the buried chest on the treasure map.

A mystery, X is. Just like the blue car.

♦ ♦ ♦

As we have noted, Winter's job is filled with routine, and this allows him to daydream from time to time, giving his imagination a chance to work. When things get relatively dull he finds himself imagining the stories behind the claims he receives, to conjure up the truth of what really happened to cause the accidents and other claims he processes. For each claim is a drama in miniature, presented by the claimant, and sometimes it fails to match up with the facts. These are the times when Winter takes matters into his own hands, to imagine what the truth might be.

And it is not just those people, but the people he sees each day, walking on the way to work, passing by the window of the automat where he has lunch, sitting next to him on the bus on the way home. Sometimes, when he is sitting on a park bench or standing at a stop sign or reclining on the sand at the beach, he will speculate on those lives—the woman feeding bread to the pigeons, the elderly man walking alone, the young couple with eyes only for each other, to whom there is no problem in the world that cannot be overcome. After all, everyone has a story, and for ninety-nine percent of those people, the story will remain untold. These, too, are stories that Winter yearns to know, but he understands that the truth will always remain incomplete.

Now, at home late at night and faced with a mystery that keeps him awake, he starts to speculate on what happened to the X man, the owner of the blue car. One theory runs into another until he can no longer keep track of them, and so eventually he gets out of bed and settles into a chair with a pen and the yellow legal pad with the green cover, and begins to consider the various options in order, starting with number one.

CHAPTER 5

*T*he most obvious answer is that X is in his home, unable to get out, dead or dying. He is an older man, a widower living alone, perhaps with a history of health problems, and one night while he is watching Sid Caesar on television he feels a pain in his chest. He has been an active man all his life–physical labor, working with his hands in a factory or plant, not to mention his time in the army–and seldom has a day gone by without him suffering some type of ache or pain. But men of his generation don't complain about every little thing that comes up; they just live with it. Why, just that morning his trick knee starts to act up, and X knows that a cold front is about to change the weather. Besides, Caesar has been particularly funny tonight and X is probably uncomfortable from laughing while sitting in the chair parked in front of the tube. He just needs to get up more often and move around.

When the pain does not immediately subside, X changes tack: it wasn't from having laughed too hard, but heartburn from dinner. Having lived alone for the last few years, X has learned to put together some basic meals, but he is not a gourmet cook by any means, and it would be a stretch of the imagination to suggest that he has anything approaching a well-balanced diet. So it's just something coming back to haunt him. Yes, that's what it is.

But not only does the pain not decrease, it actually builds up, across his chest and down his left arm. Instinctively, X knows what this means, and he also knows that a decision must be made. Does he stand up, walk across the living room, and dial the operator to call an ambulance? Or does he continue to sit there, waiting for the pain to increase in intensity, knowing that if he does nothing the end will soon be upon him?

He has faced pain many times in his life, both physical pain and the personal pain of his wife's death. And while the physical pain is often of a temporary nature, the personal pain lasts much longer. There is seldom a day in which he does not think of her–Therese was her name–and their life together. Her death left a gaping hole in him, and he wonders now if the hole is ready to be filled. People have always feared death, but for him death is nothing more than an end to that which has given him the most pain. Beyond death there is Therese, waiting for him, and if that is the case then how awful can death really be? After all those years–he can almost imagine her standing there, in the dress she used to wear to church on Sundays, waiting for him to join her. Is that not worth a little pain in the short-term, for the happiness that is to follow?

The decision having been made, he sits there and waits, and as it does the pain increases, but it is only temporary. Like everything else in life, in this world, it will not last.

There are variations to this theme, of course–X chooses life, tries to get up to call for the ambulance, but is unable to make it to the phone. He collapses onto the rug in the living room, the television continuing to prattle on in the background while the last moments of his existence ebb away.

Or it could be that X is an eccentric, one of those who lived through the depression and the bank failures and ever since has refused to trust his money any place where he cannot see it. It is the hoariest of clichés to suggest a mattress stuffed with greenbacks, but even in a small flat such as the one in which he lives, there are plenty of places to hide a substantial sum of money without ever really letting it out of your sight.

That is the rumor, at any rate, that has circulated among the neighborhood boys, the toughs and gang members who prowl the streets at night using the trash-strewn alleyways as their citadels, gathering to initiate new members into their secret society. It is typical that those who deign to seek such admittance are asked to perform some particular act of fealty, a demonstration of their trustworthiness and dependability–qualities that are especially prized in this closed circle of young boys aping their heroes in the movies. Take Taylor, the troubled kid who's fallen in with the wrong crowd. His quest is to break into the old man's home and find the loot that everyone figures he's stashed somewhere. Late that night, dressed in dark blue clothing (because he has nothing black in his closet), he creeps up the fire escape and carefully, quietly, slides open the living room window and eases himself through the small space, figuring X will be asleep at that hour. But as soon as he hears Steve Allen's Tonight Show from X's bedroom, he knows he has made a disastrous mistake. Before he can even think twice, the old man is on top of him, showing surprising strength, and Taylor even begins to fear for his own life, not knowing what this crazy old fool is capable of. Perhaps at that point he lashes out at X, knocking him off balance, or it could be that in attempting to spin out of his grasp, X loses his footing and falls back. Whatever the reason, X strikes the back of his skull on the corner of an end table, and begins to bleed heavily onto the carpet.

Taylor hesitates, panic-stricken, but he knows there is not much he can do. He could call the police for help, but that would be as much as cooking his own goose, leaving him virtually no chance for escape. (This is not necessarily true, of course, but the combination of Taylor's youth and the extreme fear that now grips him makes it impossible for him to think clearly.) Besides, X's head wound is so massive (or so it appears) that X is either dead or will be shortly. He's almost beyond help already, Taylor tells himself.

With a genuine sense of regret, the boy moves quickly and silently, retracing his steps to the window, and from there down the fire escape and into the shadows. He will spend much of the night retching his guts out, sobbing like the kid he truly is, mourning the loss of two lives: X's, and his own.

As for X, there is not much more that can be said. Whatever the reason, regardless of the circumstances, his story is coming to an end. There is nobody to call on him, nobody to look after him, nobody to notice that he is no longer where he is supposed to be, because he is supposed to be nowhere, he is supposed to fade into the background, and that is what he has done and none are any the wiser. The open window spares his neighbors the stench of death, at least for now. The truth will emerge, eventually, but for the time being the present is all that we have, and so we leave X on the floor in his apartment, his eyes open but no longer seeing, his car destined to remain where he last left it, impassively, showing no emotion.

CHAPTER 6

It makes sense, Winter concedes, but the scenario doesn't really satisfy him. He would like to think there is something larger and more mysterious out there that provides the explanation.

For example, X is actually a younger, less passive man. He is, in fact, a small-time crook who does odd jobs for a mob boss. X is not a brilliant man, at least as far as formal education is concerned; orphaned at an early age, a survivor of the war, come home to a future without much potential. He has enough native intelligence to stay alive, however—X is nothing if not a survivor.

Shortly after he returns to the States from Europe he meets up with Baxter, a friend from the days before the war. After getting reacquainted over a brew at the corner bar, Baxter asks X what he is up to. Got much going? Nothing, X answers with a shake of the head. For guys like me, things haven't changed much.

You know, Baxter says after taking a quick look around to make sure he isn't overheard, if you're interested, a friend of mine has a business he might be able to use you in. The pay isn't spectacular but it's steady, and the work isn't too bad as long as you're willing to not ask too many questions. He might be able to help you out if you're interested.

Of course I'm interested, X replies. Who wouldn't be?

So Baxter introduces X to his partner, Taylor, which serves as X's introduction to the world of the mob. X starts out running errands for the boys who run the numbers racket, just enough to prove his loyalty and trustworthiness. Having demonstrated his dependability, he eventually graduates to more important duties within the organization. Always, however, he makes sure there is no killing involved in what he does, and only as much violence as might be necessary.

Soon enough, X comes to understand the truth, that he is a relatively low man on the totem pole and is likely to remain there, but having come up through the school of hard knocks he believes this is probably the status in life he deserves. No better, no worse. Besides, he knows enough about how the mob works to understand that ambitious men often meet violent ends if they're not careful, and X isn't nearly ambitious enough for any risk to be worth it.

Eventually this changes, and as is often the case in situations such as this, it changes because of a girl. Her name is Trixie, and X first encounters her while making a pickup at a restaurant in which Taylor has a stake. Trixie works there as a cigarette girl, and from the moment X first lays eyes on her, he is hooked. To say that it is love at first sight is not only a cliché, however, it is an exaggeration. For X it is animal attraction, pure and simple.

The rest of the story is a familiar one. Trixie is a girl with expensive tastes, and soon X finds himself unable to keep pace with them. Desperate to do whatever it takes to keep Trixie's interest (for it would be too easy to lose her to someone more interesting that a small-time runner), he begins to skim from the top of Taylor's profits. X harbors no illusions that he will get away with this scheme; he knows there will be no escape, that death will eventually catch up with him, but he is powerless to resist. He has seen the horrors of war, he has experienced the kill-or-be-killed moments, and after that any risk would be worth it to bring life back to his lifeless existence. Perhaps in the back of his mind he knows Trixie does not love him and never will, that she loves only her own youth and the baubles he provides her, and that once these are gone she will be as well. If that's the way it is, he thinks, so be it! Live only for the moment, and don't worry about what tomorrow may bring, for it may not come at all.

By this time he's had more than a few to drink, sitting at the same bar where Baxter introduced him to all this, mulling it all over on the very stool where his unholy alliance with Taylor first started to take shape. Tomorrow may not come at all! he says out loud several times, his voice getting progressively louder each time.

Quiet, Charlie the bartender tells him. Keep saying crazy things like that and people are going to notice.

What difference does it make? X replies. What difference does any of it make?

In the business you're in, Charlie says, it's not good to be noticed. Take my word for it, friend. You want to keep a low profile.

How about six feet under? X says in a resigned tone of voice. Is that low enough for you?

Cut to the final scene. Taylor and his boys have finally caught up with X, pulling him out of the blue Chevy as he pulls up outside Trixie's place, and the goons have administered a fearful beating in the alley. Now they drag him to his feet, holding on to him by his arms, poised to snap them in two if he tries anything stupid, and Taylor steps forward from the shadows.

You know what happens to people who cross us, Taylor says.

X nods, blood dripping from his mouth. He doesn't even attempt to fight back.

Taylor makes a motion with his right hand. Take care of him, boys, he says.

They take him to the docks, where X knows he'll be fitted for a pair of cement overshoes. Before, he'd stubbornly insisted that Trixie was worth it, that life was essentially meaningless anyway; but in these last moments he reflects on how his parents must have looked at him as a newborn and thought of all the promise and potential that existed inside him, wondering to themselves what this child would become, and how it has all come to naught. He begins to struggle, wanting at last to cling to these final shards of life, or perhaps hoping the goons will be forced to knock him out and thus spare him the final agony of feeling the water fill his lungs as he plunges into the dark abyss below.

And that is the way it happens.

CHAPTER 7

Except it happens like this:

X is not a small-time crook, but a teller in a bank, possibly the very bank in which Winter does his own business. And the temptress in this case, the *femme fatale*, is not a woman, but a filly: Golden Hind, the 36 to 1 shot that fails to pan out and puts X in the situation he now finds himself.

In this scenario X is far from the shell-shocked, disillusioned war vet. Instead, he is a clever but timid man, lacking belief in his own abilities, nervous in the outside world, content to live in an environment of mathematical symbols. For him there is something satisfying in the world of money. There are no shades of grey when it comes to counting the cash on hand in the drawer and balancing the day's accounts. He hasn't always succeeded at understanding the nature of man, but he knows that two plus two does not equal five, and the knowledge gives him comfort.

He is a conservative man by nature, having saved assiduously in order to afford the blue Chevy, and he takes good care of it, knowing that a car is an investment as much as it is a means of transportation. He keeps the car neat, much as he does the small studio into which he moved upon his mother's death.

Under these circumstances, it can hardly be a surprise that when X falls off the wagon of cautious living, he does it in a big way. For a man who takes pleasure in numbers, it also cannot be a surprise that the world of horse racing will provide the poison which he self-administers.

It starts out as a joke almost, a friend taking him to the track. There's nothing risky about a two-dollar bet, after all, is there? And when the bet pays off (Frogmaster, at a surprising 20 to 1) it seems logical to X that the best thing to do is to reinvest the winnings in another bet, and continue in that vein until the money runs out. Nothing gained, nothing lost. Leave with what you came with.

Needless to say, things don't quite work out that way. After several hundred dollars won, there will be several thousand dollars lost. The trips to the track are replaced by noontime excursions to the betting parlor that Taylor runs in the backroom of a dry cleaning shop. At first his credit is good, since he has been a regular and reliable customer, but as his luck begins to change, so does his standing among the bookies. Golden Hind is, everyone agrees, the last straw.

X is now in a spot, made worse by the inability of

those working for Taylor to understand just what a spot it is. X knows that he is only one bet away from clearing the books, and after that he will never place another bet again. His account will be paid off, Taylor and his associates will be happy, and that will be that. But they seem incapable of grasping the fact that without the chance to place that bet, X will never be able to pay them off. They can cut off his credit, they can threaten or even kill him if he continues to fall behind on payments, but neither of those actions will get them any closer to getting their money back. Why don't they get this?

Taylor himself hates getting in the middle of such disputes, preferring to leave this to his associates, but finally the time comes for him to make an appearance. And when he is done, when X has assumed a milky white complexion and every piece of clothing on his body is drenched in perspiration, the ultimatum has been presented: X has seventy-two hours to pay off what he owes, to clear his debt, or else. What that *or else* means is not, Taylor insists, for him to say. I can promise you this, though, he says, it won't be pretty. And neither will you.

The saying *desperate men do desperate things* presumably comes from a situation similar to that in which X now finds himself. His mind races wildly, thinking first of the most absurd, the most unrealistic alternatives. But he has no rich relatives to murder, no wealthy friends he can rob, nobody he can approach for a loan. In fact, there is only one place he knows of that has the kind of money he needs in order to save his life, and as he plans it all out he is surprised he didn't think of it right away.

The operation itself is simple for a clever man such as X, someone familiar with money and the way the bank operates, a loyal employee whose loyalty has been rewarded with increasing levels of trust. It's possible that X has even considered such a plan in the past, a mere intellectual exercise of course, but if so it would explain why he was able to put it into action so quickly. Quicker than he might have preferred, maybe, but when one potentially has only seventy-two hours to live, one often has to cut corners. He calculates the amount he needs, adds what he thinks of as mad money just in case, and by the time he leaves work at the end of the third day, the deed is done.

Taylor is satisfied, and possibly a little surprised. Perhaps he also suspects how X was able to pull it off, but he has his money and as far as he is concerned that is the end of that. X knows that one obstacle is down, but another is yet to come. And when it is announced that the bank examiner will be arriving the following week, it merely confirms in X's mind what he has already known will be the last act in this drama.

Get out of here, Taylor snarled at the conclusion of their business, and it is advice that X decides to take to heart. By the time the examiner has looked at the books, by the time the manager notices that X has not shown up for work, by the time the police have broken down the door to his apartment, X is on a Greyhound bus to Mexico. By the

time the woman who sold him the ticket has been inter-
viewed, by the time the bus driver has been located and has
identified the picture, he is a small resort city just off the
Gulf.

Things certainly haven't turned out the way he had
hoped. The last few months have been nothing short of a
living nightmare. He doesn't know how, but he hopes
someday to be able to make amends for the wrong he has
done. But he knows this much: he is alive, and it is good to
be alive. And that is the truth.

CHAPTER 8

U *nless it isn't.*

Suppose X is not the small-time crook, nor the good man gone bad. Suppose he is not the employee, but the employer? The owner, in fact, of a small downtown tobacco shop.

X's shop is across the street, in the Doctors Professional Building, right across the street from where Winter works. (The time has not yet come when the irony of a tobacco shop in a medical building is apparent.) A small shop, but it offers X and his wife a comfortable life. It has always been his dream to go into business for himself, and when his friend Baxter first talked to him about taking over the shop, X was more than willing to listen.

Trixie the vixen has become Teresa, X's wife. A woman concerned with managing the household budget, she has been skeptical about the enterprise from the beginning. But then she has never shared

X's enthusiasm for Baxter, always looking at him as an un-educated man, lacking the refinements that often make the difference for women. At first she tried to be polite when listening to Baxter's crude jokes and his harsh laugh, but after a while she didn't even try to pretend, and eventually she managed to arrange to be absent whenever Baxter stopped by.

And so it is no surprise that Teresa offers less than an enthusiastic reception when X comes home one evening with the proposition that Baxter has presented him. You're a fool if you say yes, she tells him, but then I suppose you've already gone ahead and done it anyway, regardless of what I might think. It's not the first fool thing you've done. About this she is right; X has the dream in his eye, the bit between his teeth, and no matter what practical objection Teresa might raise (it'll take all our savings, the boom can't continue forever, what do you know about the tobacco business anyway), his mind is made up. The next day he and Baxter shake hands, and the deal is done.

However, to the surprise of Teresa, and perhaps X as well, the business turns out to be a success. (Tobacco is hitting its peak of popularity in the post-war era, with tens of thousands of GI's hooked from the free cartons they received in their rations, and has not yet acquired the stigma it will eventually have.) Not a major success; he's not about to become a millionaire overnight. And it is hard work, make no mistake; X spends many hours at the store building up the clientele in order to make ends meet. But the shop brings in enough to enable the two of them to live comfortably. Enough for X to eventually hire an assistant to help him run the store.

One day X turns to that assistant, Tim. Look at it out there, Tim. What a beautiful day. I think I'm going to sneak out of here a little early. Why don't you go ahead and lock up when it's closing time?

It is Tim's first time closing the store by himself, but X assures him there is nothing to it. He shows him how to take the day's proceeds and drop them off in the night depository at the bank down the street, how to activate the burglar alarm and then lock the main door for the night. He then pockets a quarter he's been carrying around absently for the whole day, and strides out the door.

He knows he has invested far too many hours building the business, and thinks that with Tim now in the fold, perhaps he will be able to scale back the amount of time he spends behind the counter and in the stock room. Eventually, if the business continues to grow, he might even be able to make Tim a partner, on the way to selling him the business in much the same way as Baxter had sold it to X.

He thinks he will surprise Teresa, those stolen moments that meant so much. Perhaps they will go out to dinner and a movie, the way they did when he was wooing her, a dozen years ago. Now with the business comfortably on its feet, there are many things that can change. Maybe he can make her happy, something he seems to have been unable to do for years.

Strolling through the front door of his house, he is greeted by a strange stillness. Music comes from the radio in the living room, but there is nobody around to listen to it; dishes from breakfast still sit in the kitchen sink. X thinks to walk up the stairs to see if Teresa is perhaps in the bedroom taking a nap, the way she sometimes does in the afternoon, worn out from keeping the house. Or perhaps she is ill, he thinks, reminded of the dirty dishes in the sink. The stillness continues, the only sound that of the floorboards creaking under his step.

Reaching the top of the stairs, X can see the bedroom door closed, but not all the way shut—there is enough of an opening into the room for him to see and hear what is coming from inside. He hears what sounds like the groan of a female voice, and for a moment thinks that that there *is* something wrong with Teresa, but then as he opens the door, he sees his wife, there on the bed he bought for the two of them, straddling the body of a man, her hands pressed against his chest as she leans back, her breasts bouncing to the rhythm of her movement.

So stunned is he by this sight, he fails for a moment to recognize it is Baxter that Teresa is riding, the two of them oblivious to his presence, bodies glistening with sweat, lost in their mutual passion, bedsprings creaking under the pressure of their thrusts, up and down, up and down.

As he stands frozen in place he hears her saying, Take your time, he won't be home for a couple of hours yet, *darling.*

Darling! What is a man to do?

We've seen it all before, the scenes in the movies, some played for humor and some for pain: the cuckolded husband, the wife pulling the sheets over her breasts, the brash lover hopping around on one leg trying to put his pants on.

What is X to do?

Does he run, does he turn and retrace his steps, down the stairs, out the front door, determined to put behind him the shattered remnants of his former life? Or does he leave a calling card behind?

You little shits, is what he finally says.

He reaches inside his coat pocket for the revolver he carries for protection, because a shop owner can never be too careful. Is it him or is it her? Does he kill Baxter, the man who put him up in business while he made love to his wife? Shot dead in the heat of passion with a single bullet to the chest, while Teresa screams in terror, repeating the same words over and over, *No, no, don't dear God don't, no!* over and over again, covering her face, while from between her fingers her eyes take in everything in slow, horrifying, graphic detail?

Or maybe he waits until Baxter, the cuckolder, has left, waits for his anger to swell, Teresa crying and trying to explain, tears running down her cheeks, trying to hold him, to make him listen, to make him understand, and he snaps, and that is that.

Is it a single shot, once through the heart leaving a

thin stream of blood to pool in her naval? Does he use a blunt instrument, leaving a virtual Rorschach pattern of spatters on the wall? Does he strangle her, choking the very life out of her, wringing her dry until there is nothing left?

However he does it, it is done, and all we know is that there is one dead for sure, and perhaps two.

He understands he has to make a run for it. The neighbors will report the commotion they have heard, the police will come to check it out. If he sticks around there will be questions: We understand your wife's missing. Can you tell us the last time you saw her?

He has no choice. They will be able to trace the Chevy to him, so there is no thought of using that to flee. At best, he will only be able to drive it a few blocks, perhaps to a place that gives him a better chance for his escape.

But it would be wrong to portray X simply as a cold-blooded killer. Passion makes people do strange things, things that are not ordinarily in their character. It may not be a pleasant truth, but it is a fact of life.

CHAPTER 9

But what if the facts are wrong?

X, it is true, does own the store, but it is not a small tobacco shop. It is, instead, a prosperous department store, employing several hundred employees. Yes, X has made a good life for himself through ambition, energy, brains, and perhaps a little good luck. It is, his wife thinks, a fine time to start enjoying some of the fruits of his labor. Terri grew up in a small town, the same small town that X is from, and she marries him despite the protests of her parents, who warn her that he will never amount to anything.

Well, if they could only see them now.

But what would they see?

They would see a man who is so frugal (some would say tight) that he continues to drive the same blue Chevy to work that he has driven for the last few years, despite the fact he can easily afford one of the new Chrysler New Yorkers. That is, when they see him at all, since he continues to spend fourteen to sixteen hours a day at the office, even when he has underlings who could easily do most of the work. And they would see Terri, a woman unhappy in her marriage, entrusted to run the household budget with a meager allowance, who might as well have chosen that dullard Eugene Bixby. The one her mother liked.

No, under the circumstances it is easy to understand, even if one doesn't condone it, why Terri would become involved with someone like Baxter. He represents everything that X is not: generous, attention-paying, sensual. Their casual meeting quickly grows into luncheons, and then afternoon trysts. Eventually there comes a discussion about the future.

Why can't we just continue the way we are? Terri asks.

You don't understand, Baxter tells her. I love you, Terri. I want us to be together all the time. I'm tired of sharing you with him.

Don't worry, she replies bitterly. You don't share that part of me with him.

Baxter presses her to ask X for a divorce. That's impossible, she replies. The one thing he's always told me is that he'll never give me one. He doesn't even realize that I don't want his money. To hell with that.

To hell with that, Baxter agrees, although one wonders what he thinks privately.

The lovers realize that their options are severely limited. They can continue in the current vein, as Terri has suggested. She can ask X for the divorce, hoping beyond hope that something will change his mind and persuade him to see the light. (Divorce in these days being not nearly as easy to obtain as it will eventually become.) Maybe they can both talk to him, confront him with how they feel, ask him to be decent about it–but no, that wouldn't work either. Or they can break it off, something that neither of them wants.

Of course, Baxter adds, there is one other choice.

It has to be said that Terri only reluctantly comes to agree with Baxter's plan. It is his idea, through and through. We'll make it look like a burglary, he says. He comes in and surprises the thief, they struggle, and he's killed in the process. You remember the stories in the paper about unsolved robberies in the neighborhood, don't you? The cops'll simply assume this is another one of them, one that went wrong. And that will be it. You'll collect the insurance money and then we'll be free.

Free, Terri repeats dully, wondering if that will be possible, if they'll ever be truly free after an act like this, and why he made that apparently gratuitous mention of the insurance money. But then she feels the warmth of Baxter's lips against hers, and the touch of his bare skin on hers, and the fire that this creates in her burns away any other thoughts.

Finally it is time to put the plan into effect, and everything goes off as Baxter has predicted. After coming home from the office, X proceeds to spend another couple of hours working in his upstairs study. Thanks to a pill that Terri puts in his milk, X's reactions are slower than usual when Baxter, dressed all in black as one might expect from a burglar, enters through a window that Terri has left unlocked and surprises him. There is a brief struggle, ended when Baxter delivers a mighty blow to the back of X's head with a heavy brass bookend from the desk. X crumples to the floor, blood from the head wound gushing onto the oriental carpet that lies beneath him. If he is not dead already, he soon will be, unless he receives immediate medical attention. Which will not be forthcoming.

While Baxter heads downstairs to plant the evidence of the burglary (broken glass in the windowpane, chipped wood around the frame, papers rumpled and desk drawers opened) Terri is tempted to pick up the phone and call for an ambulance, but she realizes it would be useless. The deed has been done and nothing can erase her part in it. She does not suffer from any last-minute surge of affection for X; whatever love there was between the two has long since vanished. No, the only regret she feels now is the knowledge that she has chosen a path that will change her life forever. She was right, she thinks, to mock Baxter's idea that the murder would set them free. The only freedom now for any of them is the freedom of the grave.

In the end, of course, the plan all comes to naught. The robbery motive collapses almost immediately, for unbeknownst to the lovers the police have captured the neighborhood cat burglar earlier in the evening. There are other clues pointing to an inside job, such as the shards of glass lying in the garden under the broken window, suggesting that the pane was broken from the *inside* rather than the *outside*. For all his clever ideas, Baxter was not nearly clever enough, and within forty-eight hours Inspector Taylor has made the arrests. Terri will spill it all, as one might imagine, thus saving her life while Baxter, the mastermind of it all, heads for the death house.

She envies Baxter, for all that, just as she has spent almost her entire life in envy of others, wishing she could have what they have. When others had warned her that X would never amount to anything she had seen him as a man who would someday become successful, able to provide her with anything and everything she wanted. When she first became involved with Baxter she had thought this would bring her the satisfaction that her marriage did not. And now, as Baxter faces the electric chair, she thinks of the peace that he will soon have, while she spends the next thirty years replaying the wreckage of her life over and over, every day and every night. Once again, someone else has something that she wants.

Life is funny that way.

There is something that she does not want, however, or even think about, something that nobody has thought of. Because of a complicated business transaction that X has been working on the day of his death, he found it necessary to drive to the station and take the train to a neighboring city two hours away. Rather than spend the money on a cab to return to the office and pick up the car, he arranges for his loyal secretary Sylvia, with whom he'd been having an affair of his own (it turns out he hadn't been spending *all* that time at the office working, and after all, what's good for the goose is also good for the gander), to pick him up at the station, drop him off at home, and then drive him to work the next morning.

And so the blue Chevy remains in the spot where X last parked it, unnoticed, unwanted, unloved.

CHAPTER 10

*U*nless, of course, it was all just a dream. A dream by a man with no memory of it, no memory at all.

Maybe, Winter thinks, he's going about this all wrong.

Something terrible has happened to X, all right. There is drama involved, to be sure. But nothing like what Winter has previously imagined.

X lies in a hospital bed in a town in the Pacific Northwest, far from where the blue Chevy is parked. He is suffering from amnesia. He has been involved in an accident of some kind—not in his car, obviously, but perhaps riding as a passenger in someone else's car. For this to be plausible, of course, the driver must have been killed, or knocked into a coma, or be suffering from amnesia himself—otherwise, he would be able to provide the doctors with X's name. And how likely is it that two people would both be suffering from amnesia due to the same accident?

No, X has been injured and there is nobody around who can vouch for his identity. In contrast to the driver of the car (who didn't have a chance, poor devil), X has emerged almost completely unscathed. A few minor cuts and scratches, but nothing serious except for the blow to the head, which rendered him temporarily unconscious. But when he comes to, it is with no memory of anything that has happened prior to the accident, not even what his name is or where he is from or how he's gotten there in the first place.

Every day the doctors and nurses gather around him, and he communicates frankly with them; all the while he improves physically, but remains completely unable to recall anything about himself.

The doctors are baffled by X's case. The routine remains the same.

Anything yet, nurse? the doctor would ask.

Nothing, doctor.

He still doesn't remember anything?

Not a thing, doctor.

The doctors confer, looking at X-rays and discussing past case histories and trying different tricks in order to spur X to remember something, anything. It is to no avail. X's injury is the worst kind, one that leaves no outward symptoms but does all its damage in the parts of the body that are hidden from the eye.

Soon the police, working in conjunction with the lead

doctor on the case, decide that something drastic must be done. They call in a reporter from the local paper, Baxter, who publishes X's story in the evening edition, along with a picture of him lying in his hospital bed. DO YOU REC-OGNIZE THIS MAN? reads the banner headline covering the upper half of the front page. The story begins with X's recovery in the hospital. It details where the car was found (a mountain road just west of the city), the name of the car's driver (a man named Taylor, a loner from out of town about whom little is known), the cause of the accident (apparent brake failure, causing the car to break through a wooden guard rail and down a twenty-five foot embankment, where it crashes into a tree and overturns), and the details of what happened afterward (Taylor was apparently killed instantly; X was thrown clear of the wreckage, and was therefore un-touched when the car burst into flames and burned). X re-members none of this, coming to in the hospital to find his head swathed in bandages and an attentive nurse, Therese, asking if he is all right.

X is completely lucid. He watches television and un-derstands what he is seeing (he is especially fond of Jackie Gleason's variety show), he reads and comprehends the sto-ries in the newspaper, he does crossword puzzles in ink and he has a healthy appetite. Physically, he is ready to be dis-charged. The sticking point remains the fact that he can re-member nothing about himself.

The story runs in the paper and eventually will be picked up by the press wire services, running in papers throughout the country. A little information will be learned about Taylor, although the police consider it nothing of substance. About X, there is not a peep.

And so the questions remain. What is the connection between Taylor and X, and why was X riding in the car with him at the time of the crash? Is X a hitchhiker who picked the wrong driver to hitch a ride with? Were he and X friends from school, or had they met somewhere in the past? The skin on Taylor's hands, or what is left of his skin after the crash, is leathery and callused, suggesting a man who has made a living working with his hands–perhaps he and X had been on the assembly line during the war, or on a job site somewhere during the final days of the depression, and somehow were reunited prior to the fatal crash. Taylor is not telling, and X is not able to tell–or so he claims.

At some point one of the doctors offers a bit of conjecture that X's amnesia is all psychological, that he is using it as a defense mechanism against some type of mental trauma. An event, for example, that proves so shocking that X's mind automatically attempts to block any effort at recalling it. In that case what X needs is not a neurologist at all but a psychiatrist.

It is a haunting idea, a man without a past. Without a past, how could a person truly define who he was? And what could cause such a thing to happen?

Some of the policemen have another possibility. They wonder if it is all an act, an attempt by X to deny his involvement in something criminal. They continue to press the doctors for conclusive proof that X's amnesia is genuine. At this the attending doctor throws up his hands in frustration. I cannot say to you he is telling the truth, he says to the lead detective, but I also cannot say to you he is lying. I can neither prove nor disprove his story. We must simply take the situation as it is, and see what happens.

In the end, of course, it doesn't really matter how it happened. The point is that X is now a man without a past, a man with only the vague outlines of a future.

CHAPTER *11*

And here Winter stops, because he realizes that his
story has doubled back on itself. Instead of answering questions about X, he has proceeded to ask even
more questions. Confronted with a mystery man, he
has done little more than create, out of whole cloth,
another mystery man. In doing so, he is no closer to
the answers than he was before.

He has come up with a dozen different scenarios in all–in addition to the ones we have read,
there are tales of a master criminal on the run from
the police, a tourist drowned off the coast of a foreign vacation spot, a man with a terminal illness dying in a hospice, and others–but none of them are
of any help. Neither are they particularly taxing or
original theories. They can be found in any number
of B movie matinees or dime novels at the drug
store.

Each one, it is true, has a degree of plausibility.

Each serves, to a point, to answer some of the questions Winter has raised. But in the end there is no certainty, and as we see from the final story, it becomes too easy to plummet into a never-ending spiral of mystery, a maze of questions that inevitably collapses under its own weight.

It is most reasonable, of course, to assume simply that X is dead. Reasonable, perhaps, but not satisfying, and therefore not acceptable.

There is only one way to find out what the truth is, and that is to find out what the truth is.

CHAPTER 12

*M*uch later, after everything had happened, Winter would wonder why he had become so possessed by it all, why something so detached from his own existence had enveloped him like a cancer that wraps itself around the cells of the body, insinuating itself until it cannot be cut away without destroying the very body it has commandeered. Why, in other words, should some stranger's life have become more compelling to him than his own?

He had not been able to consider this at the time, though. In order for him to have been able to answer this question he would have needed to possess a distance and perspective which he no longer had. Call it not being able to see the forest for the trees, if you like–it's a convenient aphorism for the occasion. The truth, though we may not want to hear it, is that life is full of far more questions than answers, and of necessity this means some questions will simply go unanswered. This philosophical excursion does nothing to assist Winter, however.

We know this much for certain, however: that on the night in question, Winter is working late. (His normal workday ends at 5:00 p.m.) At approximately 6:30 p.m., as he is going through a pile of papers from his in-box, he hears Ronald, the janitor, coming down the aisle. Ronald is a jolly black man (and rotund, as jolly men are often thought to be), with a philosophical outlook on life. Whenever Winter is working late, Ronald makes it a point to stop by his cube for a few minutes. Winter has come to enjoy these interludes, and occasionally finds himself making time, waiting for Ronald to show up.

They take a few minutes, as they often do in times like this, to discuss life and baseball, which Ronald insists are one and the same.

For once, the Yankees are not the defending champions, the Giants having won the Series last year behind the Say Hey Kid. But this year the Dodgers have dominated the National League since the start of the season, while the Yanks look ready to resume their customary spot in first place in the American, which means the two teams are once again on a collision course for October. While neither man has any particular ties to New York, they are like many baseball fans in that, for them, the season will eventually boil down to these two teams.

Ronald sides with the Dodgers, because of Jackie Robinson and the other black players they've recruited through the years. That Mr. Rickey, Ronald says, he done a lot for the black man in this country. Let everyone out there see that we can do the job as good as anyone. Done gave us a chance to make a difference. (This year the Yankees have their first black player, Elston Howard, but there is no chance of changing Ronald's allegiance. Once the Dodgers won a place in his heart, there is no turning back.) The Dodgers, like Ronald, are perennial underdogs, and underdogs have to stick together.

Winter understands all this and agrees with him, but nonetheless has to admit that he favors the Yankees, even though someone once remarked that rooting for the Yankees is like rooting for U.S. Steel. The Yankees may not have the outward grace that other teams have–for them, winning is a cold, unsentimental business proposition–but they more than make up for this with the grace they display on the diamond. From Ruth and Gehrig to DiMaggio and now Mantle, there has been something about the way the pinstripers perform on the field that attracts Winter. You can root for the Dodgers, he thinks, but you can believe in the Yankees. He likes the dependability, the security that radiates from this certainty. They may have finished behind the Tribe last year, but they're determined not to let that happen again. And then, he tells Ronald, you'll be back to saying Wait 'til next year.

We'll see, Ronald says. The way they been playing this year, don't look to me like anyone's gawn' touch them, and that includes your New Yorkers.

They laugh, each man knowing there is no chance of changing the mind of the other, and then, as is usually the case, Ronald launches into one of the stories that he is always telling Winter. Winter does not imagine that Ronald reserves these stories for Winter's pleasure alone; he imagines that Ronald probably tells everyone he meets during the course of the day that same story. He has never told Winter the same story twice, though, nor has he failed to get a laugh from Winter when the story was over, or to follow the story up with a short moral. Tonight is no different. The story is as follows:

A farmer is driving down the road and spots a sign that reads Mule For Sale, so he decides to at least look at the mule to see if it is of good quality. He talks to the owner, who tells him that the mule is the fastest mule alive and that it is very different from other mules. The owner explains to the farmer that the mule will only proceed to walk when the phrase, Praise the Lawd is spoken, and the more you say it, the faster he will go. To stop the mule, the owner explains you must say, Hallelujah.

The farmer decides to ride the mule to see if the owner is telling the truth. He gets on the mule and screams out Praise the Lawd and the mule takes off, the farmer then yells, Hallelujah to which the mule stops. The farmer, seeing that he is a pretty good distance from the owner, decides to see just how fast the mule will go. So he yells out, Praise the Lawd and the mule takes off. He then repeats the phrase over and over until he is really moving it along. The farmer looks up and sees he is coming up on a very high cliff that drops off to a deep canyon below, and decides he had better stop the mule. Much to his dismay, he realized he had forgotten what the word was to stop the mule. Hoping to hit the right word, he starts rambling and spouting out words:

Amen! Glory! Sweet Jesus! Amazing Grace!

He's really sweating now as he sees he's getting closer and closer to the cliff. Finally, in desperation as comes to the edge, he yells, Hallelujah!

Of course, the mule stops dead in his tracks. The farmer, out of breath and shaking from fright, wipes the sweat from his brow looks up to heaven and says, Whew! Praise the Lawd!

The two men laugh again. Ronald points out the moral of the story, which is to be careful what you wish for. Winter ends the conversation by suggesting that Ronald keep his own advice in mind, especially when it comes to rooting for the Dodgers to meet the Yankees in the Series. You'll be sorry, he promises Ronald.

He hears Ronald and his cleaning equipment rattling down the tiled corridor, and a few minutes later he, too, gathers up his work, walks out the door and onto the sidewalk, and heads directly for the blue car.

◆ ◆ ◆

It is his second trip of the day to see the blue car, and he has deliberately waited until now, after most people have left work for the day and the sidewalks are relatively free of foot traffic, to make the additional trip.

He walks with slightly more haste than usual, and as he does so he wishes he had not waited until now to return to the car, but even as he does so he knows, in his heart of hearts, that this has been the correct thing to do, that he would have been far too self-conscious to have acted immediately as soon as he noticed it.

All the same, he hopes he is not too late.

When he arrives at the blue car he breathes a sigh of relief, but then pauses a moment, as if to take stock of the situation. He knows that this represents a point of no return, that if he goes through with this, there will be no turning back.

When he had visited the blue car at lunchtime, he had noticed something. Perhaps he had caught the car at precisely the right time of the day, when the sun was shining at just the right angle in order for him to see what he could swear he had seen.

There, next to the steering wheel, right where you would expect it to be, inserted in the ignition, are the car keys. It is something that we would not be able to understand today, but at the time leaving the keys in the car was quite commonplace, as was leaving the car's door unlocked. Now, before he can change his mind, and having checked to the left and right to make sure nobody is looking, he grasps the driver's side handle and feels the mechanism depress as he presses his thumb down, and then he is inside the car, sitting behind the wheel, looking at the car's registration card enclosed in a specially-made pouch that dangles from the key.

He briefly wonders if this is all a trick, if there is someone waiting around the corner to pounce on him now that he has taken the bait, but one minute passes, two minutes, and still nobody has appeared to challenge his right to sit behind the wheel. There is but one final thing for him to do, and that is to reach around to the windshield, remove the tickets from underneath the wiper, and stuff them in his pocket. Then, though he is not quite sure why, he engages the clutch, turns the ignition, shifts the car into gear, and drives away from the curb.

All the way home he is checking the rear view mirror, making sure he has not been followed, and as he pulls up outside his apartment building, right behind his own car, he has to admit that it appears no one has paid him any attention.

It is not until now that he dares to look at the information written on the registration:

John Fabel
275½ Endicott Street

The mystery man is no longer X.
And now it begins.

♦ ♦ ♦

In his dream that night, he is standing the middle of a road with the blue car coming straight at him. At first he thinks the car is driving itself, but as it approaches he can see that John Fabel is behind the wheel and therefore he tries to shout at Fabel to stop but he discovers he has no voice. He has plenty of time to get out of the way of the car but his legs will not move. As the car comes closer it shrinks behind the bright white of the headlights, until by the time the car is on top of him it has disappeared altogether and Winter finds himself enveloped in the light, as blinding as the sun. Finally his legs can move, and he walks into the light, and into another dream.

CHAPTER *13*

*T*he next morning, having overcome his doubts (or, if he has not overcome them, he has at least been able to push them to one side for the time being) Winter is ready to step up the action. Embrace the adventure, welcome the danger! Isn't this a vast improvement on simply punching a time clock every day? Plus, for all that, he is still curious as to the truth about John Fabel. He wants to know Fabel's story, and he is willing to intervene in Fabel's life to do just that.

This phase will call for an acceleration of tactics, careful preparation, an increased willingness to take a chance in return for a greater award. Not that he hasn't been careful so far, but he will need to be at the top of his game to make it work.

While a couple of eggs are sizzling on the stove (over easy, with two pieces of bacon, crisp, and a cup of coffee—as you know, breakfast is the most important meal of the day), he flips his green note-book and begins making a precise list of the things he must do next and the people he must talk to. A look at the list will give us snippets of the thought process that surrounded it, and his plans for the day.

He begins with a phone call to his boss, explaining that he is feeling under the weather and will not be in today, or perhaps the next couple of days. At the telling of this white lie he feels a pang of remorse, but quickly reminds himself that he has ample sick time which he has not used; in fact, he has seldom ever missed a day of work due to ill-ness, while he knows of many people who have called in sick in order to go to the ball game, or spend the day at the beach. Besides, he reminds himself, the things he is about to do have to be done during working hours, or else they will not be done at all.

His next act, an obvious one, is to pick up the phone book and look up John Fabel's telephone number. and pag-es through until he comes to the beginning of *F*. He finds only two people with the surname Fabel, neither of whose first names are John or start with the letter E. In any event, their addresses are nowhere near 275½ Endicott Street.

This doesn't necessarily mean anything–telephones aren't as ubiquitous as they are today, so it could be that Fabel has gotten one since the book came out. It could also be that this is a new address, that he has just moved to town recently, and therefore would be too new to be listed. He might even have an unlisted number. It would cost more, but considering some of the scenarios which Winter has concocted, there would be every reason to keep your name and number out of the book. So he reaches for the telephone with one hand (while turning the eggs with the other), dials zero, and when the operator comes on asks for a listing for Fabel, first name either John or J.

Is that F-A-B-L-E? the operator asks.

No, F-A-B-E-L, Winter replies.

After a moment, the woman's voice returns. I'm sorry sir, she says, but there is no listing for a F-A-B-E-L, first name John or J. Are you sure it isn't spelled the other way.

Pretty sure, Winter says, but I don't suppose it hurts to check.

I'm sorry, she says again, I'm afraid I don't have a listing there either.

Do you have anything under 275½ Endicott Street?

Our records indicate that this is a multiple unit dwelling. Without more specific information I'm afraid I couldn't give you anything more than that.

I see. Well, thank you anyway.

Well, this is only strike one, Winter thinks as he replaces the receiver. Still, it would have been nice if that had been all there was to it, to simply pick up the phone and call John Fabel and get to the bottom of this. Fabel would probably have told him to mind his own damn business, Winter supposes, but in a way he thinks that this has become just as much his business as it is Fabel's. Considering the investment in time which Winter has made, he feels that Fabel almost owes him an explanation, and he is determined to get it once he catches up with him. That is, *if* he catches up with him, for he reminds himself that none of the scenarios he has imagined end with Fabel living happily ever after at 275½ Endicott Street.

But Winter now has the bit between his teeth, so to speak, and he is not about to give up easily. John Fabel, he says out loud, you're not making this easy on me, but I'm going to find you anyway, whether you like it or not.

Having made short work of breakfast and heads out the door, taking his keys and his green notebook. Before he leaves he tucks a few of his business cards into his suitcoat pocket, as they will potentially play an important part in his plan. He then climbs into his car and heads for 275½ Endicott Street, to force the issue for once and for all. If Fabel will not come to him, so to speak, he will go to Fabel.

It is a drive of no more than twelve minutes, and he pulls up to a parking spot in front of a four-story walkup of dark, dirty Winter brick. The steps leading up to the front door are grey cement, darkened with age, lined here and there with cracks, some sporting a weed or two. A handful of children play stickball on the streets, or draw hopscotch squares in chalk on the sidewalk, or play jacks on the stoop. He sees a young woman leaving the building at the same time that he approaches, and she holds the door open for him to enter, flashing him a smile as she does so that makes Winter wish he had a little more time to waste.

The door opens into a small foyer with a longer hallway just beyond, at least two doors on either side. The foyer contains a couple of faded pieces of furniture, a pair of old wingback chairs, flanking a small, battered wooden table with some faded artificial flowers. There is a mailbox on the wall with places for each of the tenants, and Winter scans them rapidly before finding what he is looking for: FABEL 2A, written in dark black pen on a small piece of white pasteboard.

He looks at the numbers on a couple of doors, quickly ascertains that the 2 units are on the second floor, and climbs the stairs. 2A, as it turns out, is the first apartment at the head of the stairs on the left. He knocks on the door several times, but there is no answer.

As he stands in front of the door he hears a creaking sound coming from behind and below, and then a woman's voice. It's a waste of time knocking, she says, the place isn't so big that he wouldn't have come to the door by now if he was home.

He turns around. A small woman with stooped shoulders, dressed in a housecoat that she is clutching tight to her breasts, is standing at the foot of the steps looking up at him.

What do you want with him, she continues, nodding in the direction of Fabel's door.

Are you a friend of his? Winter asks.

She lets out a short snort. Hard to make friends with someone you've never seen.

I beg your pardon?

She walks up the steps toward where Winter is standing; actually, she half mounts the steps, half pulls herself up by the banister. As she arrives at the head of the stairs, she speaks to him again. I'm Virginia Edwards, the landlady, which makes it my business to ask what your business is with him.

She hasn't confronted him as to how he's gotten in the building, leading Winter to think she must be used to strangers being let in. All the same, there is something in her manner that suggests Winter will not be receiving an invitation into her unit, so he decides to come right to the point. He has thought about his next action carefully, and has gone over the words until he is confident he can deliver them comfortably, or at least convincingly.

He pulls out one of his business cards and hands it to her, while introducing himself. I represent an insurance company, Consolidated Mutual. An uncle of Mr. Fabel's owned a life insurance policy with the company.

I wouldn't know anything about that, Virginia Edwards says.

No, I'm sure you wouldn't, Winter replies. Well, you see, this gentleman has passed on recently, leaving Mr. Fabel as the beneficiary to his policy. It's a considerable sum of money that's involved, and in order to complete the payment there are a few things we need to verify, as well as some information from Mr. Fabel himself.

It is one of the oldest tricks in the book, he realizes, but he's got the business card and the phone number to show who he is, and it will all hold up if someone decides to call and check up on him.

You say his uncle left him money?

He did. I can't say exactly how much of course, but it would be safe to say it isn't a sum that would disappoint Mr. Fabel. That is, if I can track him down and clear up these last few details. Do you have any idea when he might be back?

I couldn't tell you when he's coming back or when he's going out, or how many times he's done either. The rent is paid, and that's all I care about. He's lived here for five months and I haven't seen him once in all that time.

Winter finds this hard to believe. Never? he replies. Didn't you at least see him when he rented the apartment?

She shakes her head and explains that Fabel is actually subletting the apartment from the regular tenant, a man named Paulsen.

Is there any way to reach this Paulsen? Winter asks, trying to sound nonchalant,

You'd have to go a fair way to talk to him, she replies, since he's busy traipsing through Europe and Asia. The last postcard he sent me said he's heading up the Himalayas, wherever that is. Why he'd want to go climbing up that thing is a mystery to me.

Before leaving, Paulsen assured Virginia Edwards that everything would be taken care of in his absence, and he has been true to his word, having given her a check for an entire year's rent the day before he left. Fabel is apparently a friend of Paulsen's, but beyond that there is nothing Virginia Edwards can add, since she has not seen John Fabel even once. It is unusual, she admits, but on the other hand Fabel has been a model tenant. There are no complaints, no disturbances, no cause to call the police. As long as he doesn't cause any trouble, and the rent is paid up, that is all she cares about.

It sounds like he lives a pretty quiet life, Winter says to Virginia Edwards. He asks if she can ever remember any noise coming from above her, in Fabel's apartment. You must have heard something–footsteps, people moving about, maybe people's voices, sound from a radio or television?

I suppose I haven't really thought about it, she replies. I'm sure I must have–well, I would have had to, wouldn't I?

Do you know if he has any close friends in the building? Someone he might have told if he was planning to be away for awhile, maybe a neighbor take in his mail or look after the place?

Not anyone I know of, Virginia Edwards replies.

As the conversation continues, the two are joined by a third person, a woman probably in her early forties, Winter thinks. A burning cigarette is between two fingers on her right hand, while in her left she holds the morning paper.

Winter introduces himself to the woman, who says her name is Georgia Blake. My friends call me Georgie, she explains. As they talk Winter revises his opinion of her age, now estimating that while she may well be forty, she looks at least ten years older. He guesses by the extravagant way she moves and uses her hands that Georgia Blake may, once upon a time, have had a career in the theater, and continues to trade in on the faded memories of that career. If she were to invite him in for coffee, Winter thinks, it would not be five minutes before she was sharing with him stories of the greasepaint, and how close she had come to her big break, and the circumstances that had intervened to prevent it happening.

She is going on about how it was a good thing that Winter had come today because if he'd waited until tomorrow, she and Ginny would have been at their monthly Women's Council meeting, when Virginia Edwards interrupts. Mr. Winter says he works for an insurance company, she tells Georgie Blake. He's trying to get hold of the man in 2A—you know, the one where Mr. Paulsen used to be?

Oh yes, Georgie says with an exaggerated sigh.

Says this man—Fabel, you say his name is?—has some money coming to him. How much did you say it was? she asks Winter.

I was asking Mrs. Edwards about Mr. Fabel, Winter says to Georgie, ignoring the question by Virginia Edwards. Do you happen to know him? Have you seen him recently?

She shakes her head. Like Virginia Edwards, Georgie Blake has no memory of ever having seen Fabel. And I know pretty much everyone on this floor. Some of them pretty intimately, I can tell you, she adds with a wink. He's not like Mr. Paulsen, she tells Winter. Now *he* was outgoing as can be, always stopping to talk about the weather or what's going on in Washington. We used to see him here all the time. Now, I guess he's off climbing mountains or something–can't understand why, she adds, when there are plenty of interesting things to climb around here.

You have to walk by his apartment on the way down the stairs, Winter points out. Do you remember ever hearing anything, seeing anyone coming out of his apartment, anything like that? Since Fabel moved in?

How long did you say he's been here? Georgie asks.

He moved in about five months ago, Georgie, Virginia Edwards says.

After thinking for a moment, Georgie's answer, using many more words than necessary, is once again no.

We call her the floor warden, Virginia Edwards adds. If anything goes on here on 2, you can bet that Georgie will have heard about it. If she hadn't come along when she did, I would have suggested you talk to her, but I suspect she could already tell something was up, with that sixth sense of hers.

Ginny, you're too kind, Georgie says, looking down modestly.

Suddenly a cloud crosses Virginia Edwards' visage, a dark thought on the horizon. Do you think something's happened to him? she says, unconsciously putting her hand on Winter's arm. He could be lying there dead.

Do you really think so? Georgie asks, with just the hint of excitement in her voice. Maybe we should go in there and check? He could be sick or unconscious, you know. It could be anything!

The two women look at Winter, investing him with a kind of authority. The man with the business card is now the man in charge. It seems like something straight out of one of his scenarios, and in that instant he has half convinced himself that they will indeed find a dead body in the apartment, even though there would certainly have been some kind of a stench coming from the interior, unless the killer had installed an ice box.

For all of his planning, he's momentarily thrown by this unexpected twist, but recovers quickly. I'm not the police, it's not really for me to say, he begins, but you are the landlady, he says with a nod to Virginia Edwards. If you ask me, I think you have every right to find out whether or not something's wrong with one of your tenants, or if something's been going on in there.

Her mind made up, Virginia Edwards reaches for the passkey she keeps in her coat pocket. It's not as if I'm being snoopy or anything, she adds.

Of course not, Winter says comfortingly, smoothly, now completely in control of the situation.

Winter and Ginny crowd around Virginia Edwards while she inserts her key into the lock. As she does so, Winter can hear her say I hope the chain isn't set.

If it is, you'll just have to break the door down, Georgie says, looking in Winter's direction.

The key turns, there is the click of the bolt sliding

back, and then with the push of her hand, the door slowly opens, accompanied by a creak.

What is it that they see?

Looking in the room, the three of them all at once (Winter, as the tallest, then Virginia Edwards, her hair brushing his chin, and Georgie looking over Winter's shoulder) are greeted by a scene of complete normalcy, a scene which both disappoints them and at the same time leaves them with a feeling of relief. A dim light fills the room, the sun shining through the pulled shades, dust particles dancing lazily in the air, stirred up from the opening of the door.

Mr. Fabel? Virginia Edwards calls out. Mr. Fabel? It's Mrs. Edwards, the caretaker. Are you all right, Mr. Fabel?

Winter would like to barge on in, but he allows the others to take the lead. The three, grouped closely, walk through the front door into the living room, a small kitchen to the left, a hallway to the right, two windows and a small dining table straight ahead. It is not luxurious, but it is not shabby either. A bookcase, a pair of chairs, a radio, a small television set, an oriental rug, complete the tableau. There is a thin layer of dust on the furniture, enough to demonstrate that it has been awhile since it has been dusted, but not so much as to suggest it has been abandoned. The place smells empty, but not musty, not deserted.

And, thankfully, there is no body in the living room.

Nothing here, Winter says redundantly, to break the silence.

What about the rest of the apartment? Georgie says

eagerly.

They continue their way through the rooms, Virginia Edwards looking first left, then right, searching for evidence of–what? Anything out of the ordinary, but what could be said to be ordinary about any of this?

The kitchen itself looks to be neat and tidy, and the dining table under the windows is a small laminate model, with one chair pushed in to the table, facing the window. Winter notices the books in the small bookcase in the living room, glancing casually at the titles as they walk past it, but nothing is of specific interest at this time.

He does not want to spend too much time on details, though; the two women are already ahead of him, walking slowly yet purposefully down the hall, where the bedroom is on the left, a small bathroom on the right. Virginia Edwards is opening each door and peering behind it, looking into closets, checking under the bed, pushing the shower curtain to one side and glancing in the bathtub. When all is said and done, they have found exactly nothing. Not just the lack of a body, Winter notes, but the lack of a living being having been here. There are no pictures, no small touches that make a house into a home, as they say. The closet houses some clothes that could have belonged to anyone. It is totally anonymous, with, Winter thinks, all the personality of a hotel room.

He would like to stay behind, looking through drawers and on tabletops, searching for envelopes, papers, anything that might provide a clue to Fabel's whereabouts, but he can sense that this is not the time for such a request. Already Virginia Edwards, her curiosity satisfied for the time, is headed back through the living room, to the front door. Besides her Georgie is keeping up a constant stream of chatter. Well, she is saying, that was much ado about nothing. We're just lucky he didn't walk in on us when we were going through the place. Of course, we could have just blamed it on that insurance guy. Said it was his idea, you know. Oh well–I wonder what's happened . . .

Back in the hallway outside the entrance to the apartment, Virginia Edwards turns back to Winter. Well, Mr.–Winter–she says, looking again at the card he had given her, I guess you're out of luck. Your man doesn't seem to be at home, and if anything's happened to him it didn't happen here.

I appreciate it, Mrs. Edwards, Winter says with what he hopes sounds like conviction. You've been most helpful. We'll just have to keep on trying. I don't suppose you know anyone else who might be able to help?

Sorry, Virginia Edwards says.

Winter nods. He knows there is nothing more he can do here, that she would not be inclined to let him in to look around further, and if he were to slip her a couple of sawbucks, something he sees the private dicks on television do all the time, it would only make her that much more likely to remember him later on if anything were to happen–and this is something he definitely does not want.

He makes his goodbyes to the two women, handing

Georgie Blake one of his cards (or, rather, tucks it between two of her fingers, since her hands are still occupied with the morning paper and the burning cigarette) and asks the two women to please contact him at the number on the card if either of them happen to see Mr. Fabel.

I'll be sure to give him the message, Virginia Edwards tells Winter as she tucks his card inside the pocket of her housecoat.

I'm sure you will, Winter thinks to himself.

♦ ♦ ♦

Directly across the street from 275½ Endicott Street is another apartment house, which Winter spends a few minutes carefully studying, sizing up its location in relation to the building he has just left, before striding deliberately up the steps. The unit he is looking for is also on the second floor, belonging to a man named Jensen, and though by this time he doubts it will do any good, considering the lack of success he has just had, he figures he might as well go through with it, since he is already here.

Once Winter is with Jensen standing face-to-face, he tries a different tack. He tells Jensen that Fabel has filed a disability claim with Consolidated Mutual. However, CM has reason to suspect that Fabel is not really disabled, but instead is trying to defraud the company, and Winter has been sent out to further investigate the claim. With that in mind, can Jensen recall any time he might have seen Fabel through the window, moving around in his own apartment? Since you're just across the street from him, Winter says, I thought it might have been possible that you noticed something going on over there. It doesn't even have to be anything unusual—even if he were just up and walking around his apartment, that would tell us something.

But here again the answer is disappointing. Jensen has only been living in the apartment for three months. He can tell Winter one thing, and that is that in those three months, he has noticed nothing unusual going on in Fabel's apartment. As a matter of fact, he has noticed nothing at all.

I wondered if he might be out of town, Jensen adds.

What makes you think that? asks Winter.

Well you see, as you pointed out, this gentleman—Fabel, you say his name is?—well, his window is right across from mine, and that means once it gets dark, I'd notice if there was any light coming from over there. And I haven't ever seen any light from that window. What I have noticed is that when it gets dark out there, it's real dark. There's only the light from the street corner, and that doesn't really do much over here. Even if he had the blinds pulled and it was shining through, I'd be able to notice. So you see, I'd have to know if there was a light on over there, 'cause it would stand out like a star in the sky.

You sound pretty sure, Winter says.

Even late at night I haven't seen it on. I sometimes have trouble sleeping, and I get up maybe two, three times a week and come out here and stand at the window, looking down on the street. Don't want to disturb the wife, you know. See some interesting things out there at that time of night, let me tell you. Thought about asking my doctor about it–the trouble sleeping, that is, see if there was something he might be able to proscribe for me.

So you're up two or three times a week, Winter prods.

Right. And even then, there's nothing going on over there. You see, now that you mention it, even if he were working evenings and didn't come home until late, you'd expect that he'd turn on a light when he gets home. He wouldn't just go straight to bed, or at least I wouldn't. So he's not home in the evenings, he's not home late at night. I can't see too well over there during the day, but I don't recall I've ever seen anything then, either. That's how I figured he might be out of town. I guess that helps your case too though, doesn't it?

How so, Winter asks.

Well, you say you think he's faking a claim. I suppose if he's out of town somewhere, that must mean that he's moving around pretty good. That would mean he wasn't disabled, wouldn't it? And that would be good for your company.

Yes–of course, you're right.

Maybe he's a vampire or something, Jensen says, laughing. You know, sleeps all day, goes out at night. That would explain a lot.

Maybe, Winter says.

Well, good luck with your case, Jensen says.

Thank you, Mr. Jensen, Winter replies. As you said, you've been a lot of help.

Just to be on the safe side, he checks with two or three other tenants in the building, but their replies shed no light on the subject.

◆ ◆ ◆

Winter has noted that in the window of the back of the blue Chevy is a label with the name of a dealership, Carl's Cars, and this is Winter's final stop. Maybe, he thinks, this should have been his first stop. If he can come away with any useful information, anything at all, it won't matter whether it was the first or last stop.

The dealership is located on the corner for easy driving in and out, and identified by a large neon sign, flashing NEW and USED. A variety of automobiles, perhaps 60 in all, are arrayed in the lot. Multicolored triangular pennants are strung from the light poles, crisscrossing against the blue sky overhead. In the center of the lot there is a small rectangular building with a sloping roof, glassed in on three sides. In other words, a typical car lot of the time.

As Winter pulls up a man with thinning hair dressed in a plaid sports coat comes out to meet him. This, as it turns out, is Carl.

At first there is some confusion, for Carl thinks that Winter has come looking for a trade-in. A nice set of wheels you've got there, he says of the blue Chevy. And in great shape, too. Tell you what, I'll give you $500 on a trade for that, and I'll throw in a set of new whitewalls on top of it. New, used, we've got whatever you're looking for.

When Winter tells him that he is not looking for a car, either new or used, Carl then assumes he must be there to complain about the car, and he tells him that if the warranty has expired, there is not much he can do. There's a mechanic I know, works on all my cars, Carl begins, before Winter interrupts him once again.

I'm not looking for a car, Winter says, and I'm not looking for a mechanic. I'm looking for information. This car was purchased from you by a man named Fabel. I want to know what you know about him.

What for? Clark asks, suddenly suspicious and sweating. You a cop or something? Listen, we run an up-and-up dealership here. You can ask anyone. If this guy's been saying things about us–

I'm just an ordinary Joe, Winter tells him. This guy owes me money, and he's welched on the deal. I go to collect, and he's skipped town. No sign of him. All he's left behind is the car. I'll take it, but he owes me more than that. I figured if you could tell me something about him, anything you might remember from when he was here, it might help me track him down. And then he'll be sorry.

Winter wonders if the story sounds as lame to Carl as it does to him, but Carl is a successful businessman, and over the years one of the lessons he has learned is not to ask too many questions. Let me see what I can find, he says, and they walk to the office.

But for Winter it is a case of same story, different page. Fabel did indeed purchase the car from Carl's lot, five months ago, but the file yields little more in the way of information. Fabel paid cash for the transaction. There was no trade-in. He left an address, 275½ Endicott Street. And that is all there is.

What do you remember about him? Winter asks. Nothing, Carl replies. I wasn't the one who sold him the car. That would have been Decker, my top salesman. I know I approved the deal–those are my initials on the bottom of the sales form there, but that wouldn't have been unusual. Pretty much whatever Decker did was OK with me. He really knew how to make a deal, and let me tell you that isn't something you can teach. You're either born with it or you aren't, and Decker was born with it. Salesmen like him don't come along very often. I used to tell him this could all be his someday. I wish he was still here.

You mean he's not? Winter asks. Do you know where he went, where I might be able to find him?

Carl gives him a sorrowful expression. He can tell Winter exactly where to find Decker. Is he familiar with the address of St. Albans Cemetery, down past Fifth Street? That is where Decker is today.

I don't understand, Winter says. Are you telling me that Decker works there?

No, Carl says. I'm telling you he's buried there.

Decker is dead?

Killed in an accident four months ago, Carl explains, while testing a trade-in. He had a good eye for these things, knew how to size up its value pretty much straight away. Still don't know what happened. The weather was good, it wasn't like the road was slick or anything. Just drove clean off a curve and wrapped himself around a telephone poll. Police figured there must have been something mechanical about the car, since there were no skid marks, nothing to indicate he'd lost control or tried to pull out of it, but it was too badly damaged to tell.

I'm sorry, Winter says.

So am I, Carl replies with feeling.

As Winter climbs back in the car and prepares to drive off, Carl reminds him that his offer still stands. It's a great vehicle, he tells Winter. Even if your friend Fabel left you in the lurch, no reason why you shouldn't get something out of it. I'm sure we can work something out.

He's no friend of mine, Winter says out the window as he drives off.

Frustrated, Winter stops at a phone booth, one last chance, with a handful of coins. He is really fishing now, he knows, but at this point he knows he has nothing to lose, and he's almost frantic to have something to show for his efforts. He calls the police department. There is no record of a missing persons file on anyone named Fabel. He calls the hospitals. There is no record of any of them having admitted anyone named Fabel. He calls the post office. There is no record of any forwarding address for anyone named

Fabel. And with that he hangs up the phone for the last time, out of coins and out of ideas.

CHAPTER 14

*A*nd so: *having spent the entire day running around* chasing leads, Winter now he realizes that he is not only tired and frustrated, he is also thirsty and hungry, for he has been so focused on the task at hand that he has not eaten anything since breakfast.

There is something about going back to his apartment that he finds unappealing–perhaps it is that there will be little to distract him from the matter at hand, and he feels he needs to get away from it, to be around other people, to clear his head in hopes that some new ideas will come to him. This entire affair has been nothing more than a series of surprises, and every time Winter makes some headway, it seems as if he is simply inviting more surprises. He briefly considers calling the vice president's secretary to suggest they go out for dinner, and then quickly recoils from the idea. He has continued to keep his distance from her since the other night, and it is possible that she will have taken this exactly for what he hoped she would: a brush-off, an understanding that it was nothing more than a performance that was running for one night only.

It is equally possible, though, that she will react entirely differently, accepting his invitation, and he knows where this will end. A little dinner, a few drinks, and then it will be back to her place for a nightcap that will quickly turn into a tangle of sweat and naked flesh and animal impulses, and then he will be right back where he is now, filled with the same misgivings and regrets.

In the fraction of a second it has taken his mind to run through all these options, he has decided that the safest option, not to mention the best, is to stop at The Ratskeller, where he can get a beer and a sandwich, and a chance to tell Pete of his frustrations (even if he leaves out all the details), for there is nobody better at listening to a story than a bartender.

But once again he is surprised, for this time it is Pete who has a story to tell.

There are a few people present, but not like it will be later in the evening. Winter sees Pete standing behind the bar, a towel draped over his left shoulder. He takes a seat on one of the stools, answering Pete's greeting and Whatllya have with his order.

Pete takes the towel and polishes off the top of the bar in front of Winter before setting in front of him a bottle of Winter's favorite beer. On the house, Pete says.

What's the occasion? Winter asks, surprised, because Pete rarely does something this extravagant, even considering how long Winter has been coming here.

First, you look like you could use one. Second, this is a day to commemorate. I've decided to sell this joint. I'm moving on. If that isn't a cause for celebration I don't know what is.

Winter is not sure whether he should take this as a joke. Pete is a great guy, with a very sly sense of humor, but this doesn't seem to be the kind of thing to joke about. He asks Pete if he's serious.

As serious as I've been about anything in my life. I just signed the papers this afternoon, and in two weeks I'll be headed for Mexico.

But you've always been here, Winter says.

It only seems that way. Trust me. There was someone here before me, and there will be someone here after me. That's just the way things go.

Winter is genuinely surprised. He cannot remember a time when Pete wasn't here behind the bar, and he asks the reason for this sudden change.

It's not so sudden, really, Pete tells him. Doing the same thing six, seven nights a week for all this time, a man's ready for a change. It's not that I don't like what I'm doing. A man's blessed when he can make a living doing something he enjoys, something that brings him in contact with people every day. But sooner or later you get stale, and that's when you know it's time. So I decided to cash in my chips and see what else is out there. I'm not as young as I used to be, you know. There's a new frontier out there, or at least that's what they keep telling us, and I figure I might as well get out there and explore it a bit while I still have time.

Winter hasn't noticed it before, but Pete does seem to look older than he did the last time Winter was here, back when he was watching the fight with Driscoll. Pete's hair is thinner and grayer now, and he seems to have put on a little more weight as well. Would Winter have noticed this on his own, or is he noticing it now only because Pete has indirectly called attention to it? Or has Pete always looked this way, and Winter has simply never picked up on it, for all the many nights over the years he has been in here?

It won't be the same without you, Winter tells him.

Nothing is ever the same, Pete replies. Yesterday wasn't the same as today, and tomorrow won't be the same either. This bar isn't even the same as it was a few minutes ago, before you came in. Things are always changing, and that's the only thing that stays the same. Wouldn't it be dull otherwise?

Winter asks him what he's going to do.

There's this place I've had my eyes on for awhile, Pete says. A little fishing village down the coast, a real one-horse place. More mules than people, probably. But the first night I spent down there, it was a few years ago, I'd driven down there with a couple of friends, planning to cover the whole highway, drive as far as we could. We decided to crash there for the night, and there was this hole-in-the wall hotel with a dive for a bar. Being a professional, I couldn't help but look it over and think about what I'd do if I owned the joint. But then I told myself to stop thinking like I was on the job and relax. We had a few—well, more than a few I guess you could say—and it was a good thing the rooms were just upstairs, because I don't think any of us could have made it much further. Anyway, I plop down on the bed, and the mattress wasn't much thicker than a few sheets of paper, the frame creaked, the headboard banged against the wall, but it felt good. But then I find myself lying there wide awake—it happens sometimes, when I think I'm all in. So I'm lying there in the dark, looking up at the ceiling, and you know what I hear?

By this time Winter is expecting Pete to tell him about hearing the voice of God talking to him, or something mystical like that, such is the direction this story is headed in. But Pete's answer surprises him.

Nothing. That's what I heard. Absolutely nothing. It was so quiet there I could hear ringing in my ears. At first it just overwhelmed me, this sound of nothing. And then I could hear the clock ticking, and the sound of a horse somewhere scratching his hoofs against a dirt road. But for that one moment the sound of nothing was the loudest sound I've ever heard. That sound has stuck with me ever since, and I've never been able to find it anywhere else. And you know, living here in the city, being surrounded with everything, there's never any time to think, to see, to hear.

There's too much, and I'm afraid I'm losing something important in the noise, something I need to hear. So finally I decided it was time to go back down there and see if I could find it again.

It may have been a fluke, Winter says. A trick of the wind blowing the noise in the other direction. Or your ears weren't picking everything up. You had been drinking, after all. The place might be a regular jumble of noise most of the time. Or it might not even be there anymore.

That's possible, Pete says. I've thought about that. But I don't think so. I think it's still down there, and if I stay long enough and listen close enough, I'll hear it again. And if not—he shrugs dismissively—then it's still time to make a change. I'll buy the place and turn it into a brand-new Ratskeller, something like that. And you'll come down and see me once in awhile, and it will be just like old times. And there will still be all those nights, and even if I find myself a little senorita there will be plenty of chances to listen. And one of those nights I'll hear it.

And what happens when you do?

I don't know. That's what I have to find out. But something like that, something that stays with you so that you never forget, it must be something important.

You might be sorry, Winter says. It sounds like you've built this up into something so big it can't live up to your expectations.

I might be, Pete agrees. But I doubt it.

Winter nods. You know what, Pete? I doubt it, too.

CHAPTER **15**

Now he sits at the small table in his kitchen. The top is cluttered with sheets of foolscap, the notes he has been working on for the last several weeks. In the background the radio is tuned to Jack Buck and Harry Caray on KMOX, the 50,000 watt giant from St. Louis, where after sundown the Cardinals games are available to large parts of the country on the station's clear channel signal. The buzz of the crowd can barely be heard over the rattling of a metal fan that sits in the open window, circulating air through the small apartment.

Neither the radio nor the fan provide much more than background noise tonight, and Winter is barely aware of either. The story sits in front of him. It has taken him some time to believe that the dream is in fact not a dream, and that he has done what he has done. Later on, he will realize that from this point on reality becomes increasingly difficult to define, and that in fact what he has before him is as real as it is likely to get. And so at last he believes.

For the past hour he has been bent over, working steadily on the project in front of him. By taking an old driver's license of his and peeling back the cellophane, then using his portable typewriter and a piece of paper to alter a few facts, he has been able to come up with a passable representation of a license for John Fabel. It will not withstand close scrutiny, he admits, but it should be passable for normal use, if in fact he needs to use it at all.

Technically, he imagines, he is guilty of a crime, something like Grand Theft Auto. He supposes Collins could tell him for sure, but for understandable reasons he is not about to discuss it with him over lunch. The new license should help take care of this threat.

And to be perfectly honest, as is made clear in his notes from the night, it doesn't really matter to him. In his mind he has not stolen the car. If John Fabel should come forward, Winter will be more than happy to hand the car over to him. Besides, where would the car be now except for Winter's intervention? It was Winter, not Fabel, who kept an eye on the car and finally brought it back with him for safekeeping. Even as he sits at the table working, the car is parked around the corner from Winter's building, in one of the rare parking spots to be found at this time of night. No, it is safe to say Winter has no qualms about what he has done.

As he glances once again at the keys and registration sitting across from him at the end of the table, he thinks to himself that his situation at the moment reminds him of an old joke (probably one that Ronald had told him one evening) about the dog that chased the car and, having finally caught it, wondered now what to do with it. The symbolism of the joke is not lost on Winter, and for a moment he entertains himself with thoughts of just what kind of dog he is.

A bulldog perhaps, with the bone in his teeth, relentless and unwilling to let go. The Boston Terrier has always been known for catching rats, which is why they are so often present at the docks. Or maybe a beagle, a good hunting dog despite its cartoon image. A bloodhound is a good hunter as well, and the thought of it brings to mind images of a pack of bloodhounds pulling a police officer along, sniffing the ground in search of wanted fugitives. Could that, possibly, be the role he is destined to play?

And if a bloodhound is what he has become, then what was he before that? Probably not a poodle. He smiles at the thought that he might have been like the hush puppy on the shoes—slow and deliberate, doleful, perhaps even a bit timid. A more disturbing thought is that he was a lap dog—the ridiculous panting expression, always trying to please, non-threatening to anyone. Well, if that is the case, he's come a long way from being a lap dog.

He tires quickly of this game and gives up before speculating on what kind of dog Fabel is.

Caray's voice suddenly rises in excitement. It might

be, it could be, it is! Home run! Holy cow!

Back to the matter at hand.

It is only later that he will realize the audacity of it all, the risks that he has taken, how easily he had gotten in over his head. It all seemed logical enough at the time, but how dangerous it was, how much his plan came to depend on pure chance. For a man who has preferred to have as much control as possible over his life, he has wound up in a situation where he has none, and now he has come to understand that he cannot even control his own actions. Whenever a simple No would have sufficed, have brought an end to all this madness, he has always answered Yes instead. Now, he knows, he is about to do it again. But how on earth can he hope to get away with it?

He's a claims adjuster, not a detective, for God's sake. All he's ever wanted is a nice, simple life. A steady job, a nice girl, a couple of kids, a house in the suburbs with a white picket fence. Is that asking too much? He should just pack up everything he has been working on, all the pages of notes he has written, and throw them down the trash chute. He should quit daydreaming and concentrate on his work, which he has to admit he has been somewhat neglecting of late. He should let a P.I. do all the work of finding John Fabel; that is, if anyone really wants to know.

At this point a thought comes to him, one that crystallizes the entire situation. Maybe he's asking himself the wrong questions. Maybe he should be asking himself what he is really afraid of.

Is it, as he thought a moment ago, that he fears he will not–as he puts it–get away with it?

Or is it that he fears he *will?*

Fear of success is, I am told, one of the most common things that cause us to hold back. A psychiatrist (whom I was *not* seeing professionally, in case you were wondering) once told me that the fear of success is actually related to a desire for powerlessness, which allows us to avoid responsibility, punish those who have hurt us (often using passive-aggressiveness as the form of punishment), and manipulate others through our own self-pity. You probably understand most of this instinctively, if not clinically, she told me, since in your profession you become something of a student of human nature. And when it comes to understanding what motivates people, I believe she is probably right. However, it often takes a great deal more information than we have to come to that determination. We are forced to consider the facts as they are, and only the facts.

Which, come to think of it, is exactly what Winter has done. He is tired of the parlor games he has been playing, not only with Fabel's life, but with the lives of those whose claims he processes, with the lives of those he sees every day on the street. It is not enough to make things up, to make educated guesses; it is a desire for knowledge, for certainty, that is at the heart of what drives Winter.

He could have created a thousand different lives for X/Fabel, but none of them would have guaranteed he would be any closer to discovering the reality of the situation. And how close has he come? He has a name and an address, true, which is far more than what he started out with. But, he must admit to himself, he is really no closer now than he was at the beginning to tracking down Fabel and solving the mystery of the blue car. And, having become possessive of the whole thing, he knows he does not want to turn it over to anyone else.

Therefore, something else must be done.

His eyes once again rest on the car keys at the other end of the table.

Musial rips a single to right, scoring two. That's a winner, Buck says.

Someone once said that in order to understand something, you first have to experience it. It goes to follow that to find someone who has disappeared, you must disappear yourself.

It is the thought that sticks in his mind as he falls asleep at the table, and it is the thought that will be first up in the queue when he wakes up the next morning.

CHAPTER 16

*A*t first Winter thinks it is best to act under cover of darkness, but then he remembers Georgie Blake saying something about she and Virginia Johnson being at some kind of a meeting today, and he quickly realizes this will be the best time to move. The last thing he needs is for one of those nosy women to hear a noise and, thinking Fabel had returned home, would knock on the door to let him know a man from an insurance company had been asking after him, perhaps to find out if the man had gotten in touch with him.

Besides, any activity in the apartment is more likely to arouse suspicion at night—the sound of the floorboards, the lights being turned on, shadows behind the shades. In particular, he thinks it likely that Jensen will start keeping a closer eye on the front window, hoping to catch Fabel in the act and therefore collect some kind of reward from the insurance company. As I said, too many risks involved.

He therefore determines that the best time will be just before lunch, when men are at the office or the plant, children are in school, women are shopping for that night's dinner, and Georgie Blake and Virginia Johnson are at the Women's Club. He is aware that risk can be minimized, but never eliminated completely, and this is what gives him pause more than anything else. At last, however, he realizes if he does not do this now, he will never do it, and the chances he has already taken will all be for naught.

Before heading for 275½ Endicott Street, however, he stops at the municipal courthouse to pay the overdue parking tickets—like a good citizen, but also because the last thing he needs is to risk being pulled over while behind the wheel of the blue car.

He is directed to an upstairs office where parking tickets are handled. At this time in the morning there are only a few people in the waiting room, a dark, dingy area with poor lighting and a couple of rows of chairs with battered chrome arms and worn edges, and stuffing coming out from under the vinyl. Winter takes his place at the end of the line and within a few minutes he is standing at the counter, looking at the young woman behind the grill. Though it isn't even noon yet, she looks as if she has already put in a full day's work, with the weariness and a touch of impatience in her face.

Too late, Winter begins to realize that he has acted impetuously. What if it is not as easy as simply paying the fines? What if there are questions that need to be answered? He has no identification, no registration documentation, no way of proving that he is has the authority to be taking care of this transaction. He is not even sure if, under pressure, he will be able to remember the license plate number. Had the thought of this earlier he might have been able to prepare himself, but there are a couple of people now standing behind him and the young woman with the weary face looking at him through the grill, and he knows it is now or never, there is no running away from it now.

He presents the tickets to the woman. I'd like to pay these fines, he says.

She is barely interested. Quickly flipping through the tickets, she looks up at him sharply.

What were you, on vacation or something? she asks.

Excuse me? he replies.

The tickets. Didn't you notice them piling up? Or did you hope they'd just go away?

Well, I'm here to take care of them now. If you could just tell me how much I owe.

She turns to her adding machine and starts punching the keys. The longer it takes, the more convinced he becomes that she is stalling, waiting for someone to come in response to a silent alarm she has activated, a hidden switch on the floor or under the counter or somewhere suspected cheats won't see it.

He clears his voice. She looks up at him again, questioning.

If you don't mind, he says, not unkindly, I'm in a little bit of a rush.

Oh yeah? You're in a rush now, but you weren't in too much of a hurry to take care of this before, were you?

Don't blow it now, he says to himself. Stay calm.

You're right, he says to her with what he hopes is a self-effacing laugh. I just let it get away from me.

You should be more careful, she says. Isn't that the truth, he thinks to himself.

Finally she looks up at him and tells him the amount he owes. His breath comes out in a sharp stream. That was a bit more than I was expecting, he thinks. But it's true that sometimes you just have to spend money to get what you're looking for. Think of it as an investment.

He takes out his wallet and pulls some bills from it. She fills out a receipt, stamps it in a couple of places with an official-looking stamp, and hands the receipt to him.

That's it? he asks.

You were expecting green stamps, maybe?

I'm sorry, I just meant, is that all you need from me? There isn't anything else I need to give you?

You're free to go, she tells him.

He thanks her for her help.

You should be more careful next time, she repeats. Don't take the chance something might happen.

Yes, I know. It was completely my fault. It won't

happen again, I can promise you.

No need to make the promises to me. It's nothing to me one way or the other what you decide to do.

It is another strain on his finances, but the last thing he needs is to risk being pulled over while behind the wheel of the blue car.

That was a close one, Winter thinks as he leaves the building. Not that he was in any danger of being caught; it is clear to him that the woman was interested only in collecting the fine, and she was barely interested in that.

No, what bothers him is that he didn't handle the situation very well. He came close to coming apart, his nerves getting the better of him, and he realizes he will need to be much smoother, much more sure of himself, in order to carry his plan through. Act as if you are who you say you are, he tells himself, and you're where you're supposed to be. At any rate, this mission has been accomplished. He has eliminated the threat of being pulled over. And he knows he will do better the next time.

And now, he is in front of 275½ Endicott Street once more. Glancing at the clock on the dashboard of that blue car, he sees it is eleven-thirty, time to move. After everything that has happened, it is hard for him to believe it was only yesterday that he was first here. But now it is the next day. It is also both the last day and the first day.

♦ ♦ ♦

Again, Winter has a relatively easy time gaining entrance to the building. He pulls his coat collar up and keeps the brim of his fedora low over his eyes, to hide his face as much as possible. He walks up the stairs to the second floor, trying to put as little pressure on his feet as he can. Every time he hears a floorboard creak under his feet, he winces, and it is so quiet in the building that he fears even that act of crinkling up his face will make a noise.

After what seems to be an eternity (but in fact, had he looked at his watch, was actually seventy-two seconds), Winter finds himself standing once again in front of Fabel's apartment. Looking up at the transom above the door, he can see that the only light coming from the interior of the apartment is from the dull light that passes through the drawn shade in the front room. From his pocket he pulls out a stiff piece of celluloid, a pocket calendar put out by Consolidated Mutual for its customers. Carefully he slides it between the lock and the door jam, hoping to feel the lock slide. He has seen this done often enough at the movies to have some confidence that he will be able to do it himself, but he knows his time is limited. If he cannot make it happen in three or four attempts, he will force himself to retreat.

There is no need to worry; the flimsy lock is tripped almost at once. Carefully Winter grasps the knob and pushes the door inward, meeting no resistance save the creaking of the door's hinges. He curses himself that he did not think to bring some oil to ease its movements, but then he will be

the first to admit he has had no previous experience breaking into an apartment. If the occasion arises again in the future, he thinks dryly, he will be better prepared.

The scene inside the apartment has not changed from
yesterday, but then he hadn't expected a sudden return
home by Fabel. Winter isn't sure whether or not this would
have been a good thing; while it would answer a lot of questions for Winter, it would undoubtedly generate a great
many more from Fabel. But he's there to find answers, and
so he proceeds to work his way systematically through each
room of the small apartment, looking for the details that he
would not have had time to notice yesterday—after first re-
moving his shoes, so his steps will be as silent as possible.

The living room windows are shut tight, the shades
pulled, providing a weak light in the room—as Jensen had
said, it made him think Fabel worked nights and slept days—
and Winter has the sudden thought that Fabel might have
been a photographer, perhaps a taker of dirty pictures used
in blackmail. It would have been easy to imagine a situation
in which he'd had to flee in haste, after one of his schemes
had gone awry, perhaps resulting in injury or even death to
the girl serving as his accomplice. But not only is there no
evidence of photographic materials such as cameras, tripods,
lights and backdrop, there is no suggestion of a dark room
or other processing supplies, which means that whether or
not he took the pictures there in the apartment, it is unlikely
he used it as a developing studio.

Winter continues his way through the rooms, looking

for anything out of the ordinary that might provide a clue. The kitchen is neat and tidy, the cabinets sparse and uncluttered. There is, Winter thinks as he considers his own kitchen, nothing remarkable about this—a bachelor wouldn't be likely to have a great deal of dishware in his kitchen. Even if he were accustomed to cooking, it would be cooking for one. The lack of a formal dining room suggests that if he has any women friends, they probably go out to dinner or eat at her place.

But are there any women friends? He sees no evidence of them. There are no personal mementos on the tables, no feminine products in the bathroom, no women's clothes in the bedroom closet. There are male clothes in the closet, but no evidence of the closet being ransacked, no clues that bags were packed in a hurry. On the other hand, there's also no evidence that the disappearance came as a surprise either.

Winter is no longer worried about anyone walking in on him, for he is convinced that he can pretty much have the run of the place. He therefore begins to take his time going through the items hidden from view yesterday —under furniture, between the cushions, behind the books in the bookcase, everything he has seen detectives do in the movies. He sees a small desk in the corner of the room and searches through the drawers, but he only finds a stack of legal pads with green covers, identical to the one he himself uses.

At one point Winter thinks about pulling up the

shades to provide a little more natural light, but then he re-members his conversation with Jensen yesterday and realizes he can't take the chance. He stumbles briefly against a chair, stubbing a toe, and curses that his visit has called attention to the lack of noise coming from the apartment. Has he boxed himself in with his actions of the previous day, a stu-pid attempt at subterfuge that has gained nothing and could wind up blowing his cover for once and for all

It all adds to his frustration at the lack of any concrete information, and he begins to hate Fabel for not having left more of a trail behind him. It is irrational, he knows, but how can anyone have made so little of an mark on the world? He begins to yank the drawers open savagely, to go through what little information there is with sharp move-ments.

As he proceeds, he is struck by the utter loneliness of the apartment. Of course, most of the furnishings probably belong to the true owner, Paulsen, and it would be reasona-ble to assume that he has packed away any personal belong-ings, keeping them in storage until his return. He has invited his friend Fabel to make himself at home, however—for at least a year, based on Virginia Edwards' comment about the rent—and one might think there would be some trace of Fa-bel's existence. Instead, it could just as easily be a display in a department store window.

But if there were such items, Winter thinks, they would probably tell him nothing. Like everything else he has discovered so far, rather than revealing who Fabel is, they would likely make him more obscure than ever. Even were his name to be sewn into the lining of his coat and the tags of his undershirts, they would go no further in laying claim to him other than being a name, a cipher. It is worse than being alone, Winter decides, for total solitude leaves no trace, no mark of any presence. Fabel has left a footprint but nothing more, an indentation in the bed, but nothing to fill it.

Suddenly he feels tremendously exhausted, even though it is only a little after one. He imagines the stress, along with the lack of sound sleep the last few nights is finally catching up with him. Whatever the cause, he knows that he has to lay his head back for a moment and get his bearings, for not only is he tired, he is a little light-headed as well. He returns to the bedroom, where he stretches out and lays his head on the pillow, staring up at the ceiling. He doesn't remember turning on the ceiling fan, but he hears the click click click of the blades and sees their shadows as they rotate, slicing through the yellowish light filtered through the windowshades.

He turns to look at the hands on the small electronic alarm clock on the nightstand. The name on the clock is not Timex or Seth Thomas or any of the other familiar brands but could have come from any drug store. When he looks back up he sees that the room has darkened and night has fallen, although he has neither gone to sleep nor closed his eyes. He decides to stand up and walks from the bedroom into the kitchen.

Whereas he was looking for clues before, now he is just looking for a bottle of booze. The refrigerator is not heavily stocked, but neither is it completely empty. No booze, however, so he contents himself with a glass of water drawn from the kitchen sink. He walks back to the living room, taking his time now that he can see there is no smoking gun, no magic answer. It is frustrating to think that for all the risks he has taken in returning to the apartment, he is no closer to finding out the truth than he was before, and once again, despite the encouragement he gave himself last night, he begins to think he is going in the wrong direction. What a waste of time!

He intends to take one more look around and then leave, but instead he sits in the chair near the bookcase, takes a sip of the water, and puts the glass down on the end table. He then pulls a book out at random, Ship of Fools by Katherine Anne Porter, probably a book purchased by Paulsen before he left the country, and Winter finds the title particularly fitting right now.

He opens the book to the first page, and begins to read: *The port town of Veracruz is a little purgatory between land and sea for the traveler, but the people who live there are very fond of themselves and the town they have helped to make.*

Is that it, he wonders. Am I in purgatory? A town that I've made for myself?

As he finishes the first page he realizes he may as well stay the night here, for this place is as much home to him now as any place is.

CHAPTER 17

*I*n his dream he hears the drumbeat of his heart. It is a steady rapping against the walls of his chest, like water dripping against the head of a drum. And just when he thinks that he cannot take it anymore and that his chest is about to burst open, he realizes that the pounding is coming from his fists, and that he is trying to beat down a door, trying to escape from something or to gain entrance to someplace, he is not sure which, nor is he even sure there is any difference. All he knows is that the answers lie behind that door, and somehow he must get past it.

And then at once he is awake.

He is still sitting in the chair into which he settled several hours ago. It is daylight, and although he does not know what time it is, and is not even sure about the day of the week, he knows he should be sitting behind his desk in the office instead of sitting in this chair in this apartment. The copy of Ship of Fools has fallen at his feet. In the fog of sleep from which he struggles to emerge, it takes him a few moments to realize he can still hear the sound he heard in his dream.

It is coming from someone knocking at the door.

Almost certainly it is Virginia Edwards, alerted by the sound of footsteps overhead, thinking that Fabel has returned home. If she catches him here in the apartment, he will find himself in deep trouble, for there is no plausible explanation for how he has gained access other than through illegal means. He doubts there will be any way he can talk himself out of it. It means the police, possibly time in jail, almost certainly the loss of his job.

His only way out is through the fire escape. He turns to look for it and is about to make his move when he hears a male voice coming from the hallway.

Delivery man! Mr. Fabel? Are you home?

It is not Virginia Edwards–he has not been discovered! Winter is flooded with relief, so much so that for a moment he forgets he still has a decision to make–does he answer the door or not? Considering the lack of success he has had, there really is no choice. His heart pounding (for real this time) but knowing this is something he must do, he gets up, strides to the front door, and swings it open.

Standing before him is a slight young man wearing a nondescript uniform. You Fabel? he asks.

Winter responds without hesitation: Yes, my name is Fabel.

Sign here please, the man in the uniform says flatly, without emotion, thrusting a clipboard in front of him. What? Winter says, puzzled. Sign where the X is, the man repeats in the same monotone. Winter signs Fabel's name with a looping scrawl–after all, who really looks at signatures anyway? As he does so, he understands the young man standing before him is a messenger, and now that Winter has signed the proffered form, the man has handed him a flat manila envelope.

What is it? Winter asks.

As if I would know, the messenger replies, with a note of weary irritation. None of my business, not my job. Open it if you're so curious.

So much for a tip, Winter thinks, fishing in his pocket and giving the man a nickel. Gee, thanks, he starts to say, as Winter shuts the door.

Winter is not sure, but he thinks his hands may actually be trembling. The envelope is sealed, with only his–that is, Fabel's–name and address written on the front. The writing is so plain that Winter doubts any significance can be attached to it. There is no return address, no postmark–naturally, since the envelope has been hand-delivered. Using his thumb, he manages to slit the flap of the envelope and opens it.

Inside he finds an airplane ticket in Fabel's name, for a round-trip flight to the West Coast, leaving this afternoon.

For a moment Winter is stunned by this development, the breakthrough he has been waiting for, even though it was so totally out of his control, nothing other than him being in the right place at the right time. He replaces the ticket in the envelope and tucks it inside a pocket, but not after studying it, looking for some evidence of when it was ordered, where it was purchased, who might have purchased it. But there are no clues, only the ticket itself.

Looking at his watch he realizes he has just enough time to race home, grab a few things and drive to the airport. In stark contrast to the caution he exhibited when he entered the building, he now runs down the stairs, taking two at a time, and out the front door. If anyone sees him running or shouts after him, he does not pay any attention to it. At his apartment he grabs a change of clothing and a few personal items, which he crams into a small bag. And then, just as he raced down the steps of 275½ Endicott Street a few moments ago, he now races down the steps of his own building and, without a look back, jumps into Fabel's car for the last time and drives away.

There is something profoundly romantic about the idea of the open road, the thrill of the unknown which it dangles before you, if only you point your car dead ahead and step on the accelerator. You get your kicks on Route Six-Six, as Nat King Cole sings, and as Pete and Linc prove on the television show of the same name (although the show does not use that as its theme song, giving the whole thing a dual cultural identity), or you become like Jack Kerouac, living a life of adventure just by traveling where the road takes you. Robert Moses, constructor of concrete leviathans, is a national icon, and the interstate highway system promises to make such freedom available to everyone. But Winter has not read On the Road, nor would he evince any particular knowledge of Moses even though he has probably seen his picture on the cover of Time; and while he has always liked Route 66 (the song and the show both), he has never given either one a second thought beyond snapping his fingers when he hears the music.

Even were Winter to consider such thoughts, however, it is unlikely that he would attach any special significance to them, and by the time the irony of it all became apparent, it is unlikely he even recalls them having entered his mind. Besides, it is unrealistic to suggest that Winter has anything on his mind other than the task that lies ahead of him.

He knows that if he catches a few breaks he will just have enough time to find a place to park and catch the flight. But first he must wrestle with the midday downtown traffic on the road to the airport, and with time at a premium he makes but one stop—at the bank, where for reasons he cannot explain he withdraws all the money in his account and puts it in his wallet.

The trip to the airport passes in a blur, as Winter's mind races along a parallel track. He keeps one eye first on the speedometer, then on the clock, then on the speedometer again. He must make it in time, but he doesn't want to take the chance of being stopped for speeding. Not once during the drive does he ever consider how he will explain this to his boss or the others at work. He has decided he will let the chips fall where they may.

It is noteworthy that at no time does Winter seem to have had any qualms about impersonating Fabel on the flight. From the moment he opened the envelope and discovered the ticket, his mind appears to have been made up. One could, I suppose, argue about the significance of this, whether it represents a dramatic change in Winter's behavior. Yes, it is a decisive act on his part, after which there will be no going back, but it is also a logical act. Having first stolen Fabel's car and then broken into his home, there is no reason to suppose that he would have any qualms about taking the ticket. One can even argue as to whether or not there is, in fact, anything wrong with what he has done, for in pursuing the truth one often has to cut corners.

At the airport he passes through the ticket line, handing the attendant his ticket, or rather, Fabel's. He walks along the tarmac along with the rest of the passengers waiting to board the plane, its silver metallic surface glistening in the early afternoon sun. As he mounts the stairway he is greeted by a stewardess. Good afternoon, Mr. Fabel. Once on the plane and strapped into his seat (next to the window), he is able to breathe more easily. If he were going to have second thoughts this would be the place to have them, before the plane takes off and it is too late. But if there were any such temptations, he pushes them out of his mind, focusing on what is to come.

For one thing, and this is something that he has not yet begun to deal with, he must figure out what he will do when the plane lands. He has never been to this part of the country before. He does not know anyone there, is not at all familiar with the area. Does he rent a car? Take a cab? And where will he go? What, exactly, does he hope to accomplish with this foolish venture? Here he is, flying halfway across the country with nothing more than an airline ticket and a bag containing a few items of clothing, and even the ticket does not really belong to him. He has put his job at risk, disappearing like this with little notice. For the first day or two they will assume he is still under the weather, but after that they may call or come by and check on him—especially the vice president's secretary, who undoubtedly still keeps an eye on him. What will happen when they find him missing, though? They might suspect foul play, but eventually they'll get tired of this game he is playing, and that will be the end of it.

And for what? What will this insane trip prove? Defiantly, Winter pushes back against his own doubts. A man is missing. This is a tangible fact—the existence of the car is proof enough of that. Another fact: the airline ticket waiting for him at the apartment. Had Fabel been planning to take the trip, there is no way he would not have been around to pick up the ticket. Therefore, something has happened to him. And Winter feels that in a way he has been chosen to preserve Fabel's memory, to seek some kind of justice for him. He realizes that by thinking in these terms he makes it sound as if Fabel is already dead, and it is true that he does not know this for a fact. But there is, he is forced to admit, every reason to think this is the case. And if it is, then it is the longest of long shots that this trip will answer any of the questions.

However, it is also true that the more Winter learns about Fabel, the more he will be able to fill in the blanks, and perhaps that will shed some light on the whole matter, regardless of the outcome. If that is the case, Winter owes it to Fabel to follow the trail; he thinks that Fabel would be pleased by the actions Winter has taken. He wouldn't mind Winter impersonating him; far from it, he would be touched that this stranger has taken enough of an interest in his own life to go undercover, as it were, to find out the truth. It is even possible, Winter thinks, that he and Fabel could wind up as good friends as a result of this. He imagines a friendship filled with gratitude, or with knowing chuckles at what a big misunderstanding the whole thing was. (All the time glossing over the intense hatred he had felt for Fabel just the previous night.) Either way, a bond will have been forged between the two men that will be unlike the ties that bind most friendships. If, that is, Fabel is alive.

Soon the plane is taxing down the tarmac of the runway, and not long after that it is soaring above the clouds, headed toward its destination. It will be a long flight, lasting several hours, and Winter feels he can finally relax; for better or worse, he is now on his way, and there is no turning back.

No sooner does he close his eyes, however, when he hears a stirring coming from the front of the plane, and two men in uniforms emerge from behind the curtain separating the passengers from the cockpit. Heading down the cramped aisle, they stop in front of him.

Mr. Winter? one of them says?

Before he can stop himself, he hears himself answering. Yes?

I'm sorry, the other one says. You're on this plane without authorization. You'll have to go.

The two men take hold of Winter, lifting him up and out of his seat by his arms. Wait, he cries, what are you doing? The passengers aren't paying any attention to the commotion; they are all looking straight ahead, wearing dark glasses of the type one sees in theaters where 3-D movies are being show. The two men drag Winter to the back of the plane, where a stewardess waits for them. She opens the door, the one through which the passengers walked when they boarded the plane, and Winter can hear the wind whipping past his face.

Without breaking stride, the men rear back and fling Winter out the door and out of the airplane. For a moment everything is suspended in mid-air, the slowest of slow motion, the propellers not even moving as quickly as the second hand on a clock, the plane hanging as if it were about to fall out of the sky at any moment. Winter's arms and legs are contorted like a marionette suddenly cut from its strings and sprawled on the floor, and though he is so close to it, able to see every rivet, every indentation on the plane's metal skin, he too is moving at the same slow rate, thus the plane will always remain just out of reach no matter how hard he strains to catch up to it.

He feels a scream well up, each syllable being formed in his throat, but the words are unable to escape, trapped in his mouth, blown back down his larynx by the force of the wind. Below he can see ribbons of road forming labyrinthian paths against the patchwork quilt of farmland, maxes from which there can be no escape. And although he cannot fee himself moving, plummeting toward the ground, he can see the squares rising up as if to meet him, and if everything else is moving at half speed, the ground appears to be rising at twice the normal rate, three times, and then—

He sits up with a start.

He looks around, shaken, but he is still in his seat, the belt strapped around his waist. Everything is as it was just a moment ago. He must have nodded off briefly and dreamt the entire nightmare, but although his mind understands this, his body takes longer to comprehend the reality, to slow down his breathing and heartbeat until he is back to normal. It is a reminder of the anxieties that still dwell within him and the need to control them, but also that he must remain on the alert to prevent any slipup, any revelation that he is not who he says he is, or that he is who he says he is not.

The flight is a long one, lasting several hours, but even though it cannot be said that time flies, the remainder of the trip is reasonably uneventful. At regular intervals the stewardesses pass through the plane offering refreshments and, later in the flight, a dinner consisting of a spinach salad with water chestnuts and bacon bits, an entrée of roast rib of beef au jus accompanied by oven-warmed breads, sour dough rolls and biscuits, and a dessert of French vanilla ice cream topped with butterscotch sauce. My, air travel certainly has changed, hasn't it? Perhaps it only sounds better than it was.

In-between these welcome interruptions, Winter looks out the window and catches glimpses through the clouds of the land below. As he does so, he wonders about the lives of the people there, what they are doing and whether they look at the plane flying overhead and wonder the same thing about its passengers, what they are doing and where they are going. He hopes by concentrating on what he sees passing below him, he might be able to focus his mind on what needs to be done, but he finds himself continuing to push away any thoughts of the future, even as he has cast away any thoughts of the past. He has only this moment in which to live, for the present is all there is that is for certain.

Eventually the fatigue catches up with him once again, his head nods against the window, and he again falls asleep, this time a deep and restful one. In his sleep he dreams of a rolling green pasture, surrounded by a stone fence and evergreens. Below him the country passes by, including green pastures, stone fences, and evergreens.

CHAPTER 18

*B*ecause of the time difference, it is still only late afternoon when Winter's flight touches down on the West Coast. Winter can hear the turbines winding down as the plane taxis to the gate. Finally they whine to a stop, and he joins in the jostling as people reach up to remove their luggage from the storage bins.

The same stewardess who greeted him as he entered the airplane thanks him for having traveled with them today, and hopes to see him again soon. Holding his overnight bag in his right hand, Winter sets off with the other passengers, down the slight incline of the jet bridge to the arrival area inside the terminal. Upon entering the area, he is greeted by a blast of cool air, and the controlled environment suggests to him that the weather is hotter than it was when he left home, although he has not yet had the opportunity to experience the fresh air of the outdoors for himself.

Walking through the airport's corridors, Winter pauses and looks around. Travelers pass him in both directions; some are businessmen wearing suits, carrying briefcases and looking important, while others are families, traveling together on summer vacations now that fares have come down enough to make it more affordable for the wife and kids to fly to places such as Disneyland. Still others look to be students, dressed in tie-dyes and beads. To his left he can hear a group of Hare Krishnas, singing and chanting as they hand out their pamphlets and look for donations. Well, Winter says to himself, I'm here now—what do I do?

He has no idea where the nearest hotel is, what the major thoroughfares are, how far away from anything he is. As he scans the terminal, perhaps in hopes of finding a car rental agency where he might also be able to get a map of the area, his eyes light on a man wearing a black suit and peaked hat. He has long, dark hair that curls around the collar of his shirt, sideburns that come to the end of his lobes, and a bushy mustache. In his hands he holds a sign with a single word.

FABEL

At first it fails to register on Winter, but when it does it causes his heart to momentarily skip. He pauses, looks around to see if anyone else has noticed. Surely this can't be meant for *his* Fabel; the driver must be waiting for someone else. If he's not careful, he realizes he could blow the whole thing right here. He walks to a fountain for a drink of water, then stops at a magazine counter to buy a pack of gum. He looks back–still, the limo driver stands, holding the sign.

FABEL

Well, Winter thinks, In for a penny, in for a pound. I might as well see how much farther I can go. He walks up to the man.

Fabel? the man asks him.

Here I am, Winter replies with a smile.

The driver returns his smile, says he was afraid he might have missed him. They walk to the car, and the driver (who tells Winter his name is Ross) puts Winter's bag in the trunk. Not much luggage this trip, he comments. I like to travel light, Winter replies. Makes sense, Ross says, it's hard enough getting in and out of these airports nowadays.

Once in the back seat of the limo, Winter, trying to look as if this happens to him all the time, casually asks Ross where they're headed. The Plaza, he replies, apparently thinking that Winter simply meant to ask for the name of the hotel.

With this settled, Winter is able to sit back in the car. Ross tells him the trip will take about forty-five minutes through the traffic. They leave the immediate area of the airport, and the density of development eases off. Off to Winter's right they drive past what looks like a farm of windmills, their blades revolving in the wind. They are turn-ing counter-clockwise, and the cumulative effect is that of a talisman, pushing Winter forward. He takes some consolation in that, irrational though it may be. But to think that nature itself may be playing a role in what is unfolding–is that such an implausible idea?

By now Winter has developed a strategy of sorts. The existence first of the airline ticket and then of the limousine driver waiting for him has convinced him that something almost supernatural is going on. He was expected here, for some as-yet unknown reason. There is a plan; events will evidentially continue to unfold. He will simply have to react to them as they happen.

The limo pulls up at the Plaza. As Ross takes Winter's bag from the car, Winter goes up to the registration desk. He boldly proclaims himself as Fabel, and that he has a reservation. Yes, Mr. Fabel, the manager says, we've been looking forward to your visit.

Have we met before? asks Winter. To the manager's brief look of puzzlement, he adds, I travel so often, you know.

No, the manager replies, but I've heard a lot about you. It's a pleasure to have you as our guest.

Winter takes his bag, thanks (and tips) Ross, and heads up to his room. A bellboy accompanies him, carrying his bag up, and he tips the boy at the door. As it shuts behind him, he falls on the bed, exhausted–but, at the same time, elated. He knows beyond any doubt now that events are out of his hands, that he merely has to wait for the next move. And unless he misses his guess, he thinks the next move will come quite soon. No sooner do these thoughts form in his head than the phone rings. Once again his heart skips a beat, this time because of the sudden noise, but he is becoming more and more confident all the time. He strides to the phone on the other side of the room and picks it up.

Hello?

Mr. Fabel? says the female voice on the other end.

Yes, Winter says, this is Fabel.

Mr. Fabel, this is Samantha. It's so good to finally get a chance to speak with you.

Winter pauses for a moment, for this Samantha has said this in such a way that it is clear she expects him to recognize the name. He has no choice but to fake it and see where it leads.

Oh yes, Samantha, he says, trying to sound smooth again. It's good to hear from you at long last.

Yes, she replies, I wasn't sure this day would ever come.

Neither was I, Winter replies.

I'm sorry to hit you with this so quickly, she says, with you having just arrived. I'm sure you haven't even had time to wash up or unpack.

That's all right, Winter answers, I don't have that much to unpack.

Anyway, Samantha goes on, there's been a change in plan.

Winter's hand tightens up around the receiver. There has?

Yes, Samantha replies, and I hope you don't mind.

It all depends, says Winter cautiously.

We've had a problem with the schedule, some technical things, there's no need to bore you with all the details right now, you'll be able to see for yourself when you get here, if you're really interested; but, and I'm really sorry about this, we really do need you down here as soon as possible.

Well, Winter says, I'm not sure. That doesn't give me any time to straighten up–

There's nothing to worry about. The only thing that's changed is the timing. We'll run through everything else the way we agreed.

Of course, Winter says hesitantly, I should have known. But, he adds, it might take some time for me to get a cab.

I've already taken care of that, she assures him. I was able to reach Ross through the front desk before they put me through to you–I was hoping to get him before you reached the hotel, but I was too late. Anyway, he's still downstairs waiting. He'll be able to bring you here right away.

That's very fortunate, Winter says.

With that he heads back downstairs, taking his room key with him but leaving everything else exactly as it was when he walked into the room. True to her promise, Ross is downstairs waiting for him, smiling and holding the FABEL sign as a joke, even though there is nobody else in the lobby. Winter climbs back in the car and they are off once more.

As before, he tries to take mental notes as to the location, the surroundings, any landmark or physical feature that will help him keep track of where he is. For the most part, all he sees is concrete pavement, miles of freeway unfolding before him as if unrolled from some fantastic supply room. Occasionally they travel beneath an overpass, and Winter can see what look to be antiwar protestors waving signs and shouting slogans. He thinks he can make out the words Hey Hey Ho Ho, but nothing else. He notices signs for freeway entrances and exits, but without sufficient time to familiarize himself with the area, the names mean little to him. He makes a note to have Ross stop at a drug store on the way back so he can buy that map and study it. Assuming, he adds, that Ross will be bringing him back after whatever is about to happen to him has happened.

Winter has correctly assumed that events would continue to carry him along, but things have happened so quickly that he is now forced to consider other possibilities, things he could not have anticipated. Obviously Fabel and Samantha have at some point discussed the plan for what is going to happen. What if she has seen Fabel before, or has heard his voice? Just now, when they talked on the phone, she didn't act as if anything was wrong, but the conversation was a brief one, and anyway people often sound different on the phone than they do in person. Furthermore, the conversation left Winter with the distinct impression that there would be more than just he and Samantha present. What if there is someone *else* involved who has met Fabel previously? He begins once again to consider what Fabel is (or was) involved in, and invariably his mind goes back to ideas about crime.

This would create duel concerns: first and foremost, the chance someone may recognize him as an impostor; but this has always been a part of the equation, ever since he began this charade. What Winter finds much more sinister is the possibility that he, posing as Fabel, may be asked to do something that he, Winter, is incapable of doing. Winter is not, as we have seen, a stupid man. He is a cautious man, and this has prevented him from acquiring as much worldly experience as many men have; but caution is not the same as stupidity. It is more a case of ignorance, and ignorance can be mitigated by someone who is bright and can think on his feet, and we have to agree that Winter does seem to have these qualities.

No, when Winter considers that he may be asked to do something he is incapable of doing, his thoughts turn more in the direction of something illegal, something that would go against all his moral beliefs. True, he concedes, after all that has happened in the last forty-eight hours, that definition is apparently somewhat more flexible than he might previously have thought. Still, it is possible, if not probable, that he could be asked to do something that crosses the line. And then where will he be, other than facing two equally unfortunate alternatives?

Perhaps they have in mind some kind of initiation which he will have to pass before he can be considered a full member of the "gang." It is hardly a far-fetched idea, since he had anticipated just such an occurrence in the first "X" scenario, the one involving Taylor and X, which now seems to have been a hundred years ago. From the movies he watches in the theaters on Saturday afternoons, he knows that in cases like this, the one going through the initiation is often given a "shadow," someone to keep an eye on him to make sure he goes through with the assignment. Such a situation would give Winter very little room to maneuver, and might cause him to commit the very sort of thing he wants to avoid, just in order to escape.

Unless Fabel is a hired assassin arrived in town to carry out a hit. At least, Winter thinks, there's an upside to that possibility, or actually two, in that it is unlikely anyone present would recognize Fabel, and they probably would not be shadowing him while he went about his work. They would expect him to successfully complete the job, though; there is no way he will be able to avoid this.

And even if he does manage to get away, how could he ever be safe, no matter where he went, as long as they thought he was Fabel? It wouldn't be easy to go back to being Winter again, and in all likelihood if they ever did catch up with him they wouldn't believe a word he told them anyway. Even if they didn't track him down, how could he possibly live the rest of his life looking over his shoulder, thinking that at any moment his life could be snuffed out in the wink of an eye? He would have to disappear, much as the real-life Fabel has done, and once again Winter wonders if what he is describing is similar to what has actually happened.

Just when it seems as if he may be going off the deep end, he gets hold of himself. He has become much tougher over the last few days, he thinks, and he realizes he cannot afford to let his imagination run away with him. Don't anticipate trouble, he says to himself. Better to just sit back, observe, listen closely and say little. Only this way will he be able to get to the bottom of it all.

In time the car pulls into a parking lot attached to a low flat building, not unlike an old warehouse, set among a group of similar nondescript buildings. The area around the buildings looks to be industrial in nature but, owing to the time of day, he supposes, there are only a handful of cars remaining in the lot. Ross walks Winter to the entrance, the chauffer continuing in the good mood which has typified the entire time he has been around Winter. A man like that couldn't be working for the syndicate, could he?

Ross holds the unmarked door open as Winter walks through and into a small antechamber where he is met by a young woman who understands him to be Fabel. She in turn leads him to another young woman, tall and lean, with warm chestnut hair. This second woman is visibly harried and at first does not welcome the interruption, but a look from the first woman seems to suddenly change her tune, and her face lights up with a smile that Winter will always remember. Mr. Fabel, she says offering her hand to him, how nice to meet you at last! I'm Samantha.

Winter takes the proffered hand. A pleasure, I'm sure, he says. He makes note of her use of the words *at last* in introducing herself, meaning that she hasn't met Fabel before.

I'm so sorry that everything is happening so fast, Samantha apologizes yet again,. You've barely had time to get settled, and here you are.

These things happen, Winter says.

Well, you're being very kind about it all, but I hate that it gives off the impression we aren't a professional group.

Nonsense, Winter replies, continuing as the magnanimous guest.

So, Samantha says, shall we get started?

Ready whenever you are, Winter assures her, even though he is anything but ready.

They walk through the antechamber and into a darkened room. Whether it is larger or smaller than the first room, Winter cannot say. He finds himself seated in a chair, with a table and glass of water at its side.

And then a bright spotlight comes on, almost blinding Winter in its intensity, and plunging the rest of the room into an even deeper darkness. The heat from the light causes him to immediately break out in a sweat. He hears a question, apparently directed at him, coming from somewhere in the darkness:

Mr. Fabel, defend the actions of your life so far.

CHAPTER *19*

*T*o say that Winter is beyond stunned would be an understatement. He sits motionless, speechless, for what seems to him like hours. He can imagine the moon rising and setting, the sun rising and setting, the stars and the clouds and the shadows moving through the sky and across the ground in the time it takes him to react to what he has just heard. So taken aback is he that he cannot even tell if the question comes from a man's voice or a woman's. He takes a sip of water from the glass at the table, a nervous gesture more than anything else, and tries to lick his dry lips.

Even so, the video will show that it is a matter of a few seconds at most before Winter replies to the question.

What is this? he says, trying to keep his voice light in case it is all a joke. It sounds like some kind of trial.

We're all on trial, Mr. Fabel. Every one of us. Just answer the question.

This must be some kind of a mistake, Winter says.

No mistake.

But it must be. You've got the wrong man, Winter says, aware as perhaps nobody else is of the double meaning of this statement. Unless this *is* a trial of some kind, with the purpose being to determine whether or not he is who he says he is. And there is no denying that at several points during the day he has been heard to tell people that he was Fabel.

No, you're the right man. We made sure of that before we started.

I don't see why I should tell you anything. I haven't done anything wrong. And I don't even know you.

But isn't it better to talk about something like this with someone you *don't* know? And you'll have to answer the question sooner or later anyway. It might as well be now.

Why should I trust you?

We've become such a cynical society, haven't we? Next thing you know, you'll be telling me that you're not a crook.

I'm *not* a crook!

Of course not, Mr. Fabel. I didn't mean to suggest that you were. Figure of speech, if you will. Please forgive me.

For some reason, it satisfies Winter to say that he does. With the apology, Winter's attitude toward this sudden inquisition begins to soften for the first time.

And let's admit it, the voice says once again. You appreciate the challenge, don't you?

OK, what was the question again?

See? I knew you'd come around. Personally, I think you're stalling for time, but very well: the question is, Defend the actions of your life.

His face is a study in concentration. Between the heat generated by the light and the stress of the situation, he begins to perspire heavily.

Well? I'm waiting, Mr. Fabel.

I'm thinking, Winter says.

Really, Mr. Fabel. If you have to think that hard and that long in order to defend your life, perhaps there's a bigger problem involved.

Just what do you expect? Winter snaps, irritated once again. You bring me here, plunk me down in this chair, shine a bright light in my face, and expect me to just answer a question like that? He snaps his fingers in time to the end of the sentence. I have half a mind to get up and leave right now.

I wouldn't do that. The stakes are too high.

How high? What are we playing for?

Your soul, perhaps.

My *soul?*

Besides, you asked for it.

I did?

Of course. Why else would you accept this invitation? You don't want to let everyone down, do you Mr. Fabel?

But don't you see? It's not as easy as all that.

Why not?

For one thing, Winter says, now forced despite himself to deal with the question on its own merits, it's impossible for anyone to defend every single thing they've ever done. There are some things you do that you might be quite proud of and other things you wouldn't try to defend. Most of it you won't even be able to remember. Nobody can possibly pretend everything they've done in their life has been a good thing, unless they're some kind of saint. That includes you.

Now we're getting somewhere.

Yes, but where?

You tell me. After all, it's your life. Where has it taken you? What have you done with it? Can you answer me that, Mr. Fabel? And this time it shouldn't take you so long.

The perspiration is running down Winter's face, and he reaches up to wipe his lips with his hand.

Why don't you take another sip of water? the voice says kindly.

Winter is suddenly suspicious again. That must be it, there's something in the water causing him to hallucinate. Or perhaps it's more like sodium pentothal, truth serum, in which case the truth is sure to come out sooner or later.

No thanks, he says.

As you wish.

He now thinks the voice is female but it is so calm, so emotionless, that he still cannot be sure.

Winter comes to a decision. It is obvious there is no escape for him here, nor is there any way to shut up the voice unless he answers the question. And since he realizes there is no escape, he also understands that he has nothing to lose by letting fly.

He is being asked to defend a life that is not his—does he respond by attacking a life that is not his? Is it even true? After all, he has driven a car belonging to Fabel to an apartment belonging to Fabel, where he has accepted an airline ticket made out to Fabel, flown in a seat reserved for Fabel, moved into a hotel room reserved for Fabel, ridden in a limousine reserved for Fabel, and is now answering questions intended for Fabel. Possession being nine-tenths of the law, does he not now possess enough of Fabel's life to answer questions on his behalf? And if that is the case, it would seem that he is also stuck with Fabel's life, the good and the bad, whatever either of them may be.

But if the tables were turned, what more would he be able to say about his own life? If Fabel has not held a mirror up to the absurdity of Winter's life, then there would have to be more to it than that. Yes, he goes to work each day, he dines and drinks and jokes with others, he has lain in bed with the secretary of the vice president and had sex with her. But how much of a mark has it made? Has he been missed at work today, other than the fact that his work is not being done? They may notice that the employee is gone, but what about the man?

Anyway, what is Winter in the first place, other than an arbitrary name that has been given to designate the space he occupies in life. Does the word Winter define him any more than any other word? Say, for example, Fabel?

In the meantime, the conversation continues. Or is it an interrogation? Perhaps we haven't settled that question yet.

You were about to say something, I trust, Mr. Fabel? the voice prods.

I cannot defend the actions of my life, he says.

You mean you aren't even going to make the effort?

I mean it is an impossible task to give anyone.

That would be quite an admission, Mr. Fabel, but not entirely a true one. After all, if that were the case, you wouldn't be here right now. We wouldn't have invited you, and you wouldn't have honored us with your presence.

Well, I can't explain how that happened. You'll have to tell me. But in order to defend one's actions, he says, one must have actions to defend. What about a man who has done nothing? What does he defend? And is it always best to do something, when the appropriate thing might be to do nothing?

It depends, she says. (Winter has decided the voice questioning him is definitely female; besides, if he is going to continue this charade, it helps to personalize his interroga-tor.) But in that case you have done something. You've made an active decision to do nothing, and that itself is doing something. You might have to defend doing nothing as much as you might have had to if you had done something. But then you might as well just be engaging in a college debate society. You have to take it out of the theoretical and into the practical. How do you defend a negative, for instance? It is like trying to describe the white space surrounding a drawing—the only identity it has is based not on what it is, but what it isn't. And therefore you're trying to describe something that isn't there.

Like seeing a polar bear in the middle of a blizzard?

Well played, Mr. Fabel. I'm glad to see you've warmed to the task at hand.

Thank you, he says dryly.

But, she continues, we are not talking about polar bears in blizzards. We are discussing real actions with real consequences. I hope you're not suggesting that the lack of action means the lack of consequences as well?

Of course not. If we accept the idea that even inaction is action, then obviously it has consequences. If my home is on fire and I choose to do nothing about it, my negative action will lead to my home burning down.

In that case, your inaction is every bit as destructive as if you'd taken an axe to your home and begun chopping it down.

Yes. Precisely.

In that case, Mr. Fabel, we have even more to defend, since we must look not only at what we've done, but what we've failed to do.

That is the bottom line, he says, and in that moment he thinks he has finally come to understand Fabel as much as he has understood himself. He has been wrong in accusing Fabel of having left behind a life with nothing of consequence to show for it. In fact, one can define Fabel's actions though Winter's actions, since Fabel's inaction (if that, indeed, is what it is) is the direct cause of everything which Winter has said and done since. It is a revelation, a spark of comprehension perhaps, and he wishes he had time to mull this new theory over more thoroughly, but he knows the interrogator is still there, waiting for him to go on with his defense.

If I understand you correctly, he continues, you're proposing to judge me based on the actions of my life. But does one measure actions by results or by motives?

Explain.

The actions I have taken may or may not have had the warranted results, but sometimes that result is out of one's hands. Isn't it better to look at why I did or didn't do something, and then draw your conclusions based on the entire picture?

An interesting point. So how would you do this?

I think you have to rephrase the question, Winter says, and he realizes now he is talking not about Fabel, but about himself. What you really want to know is how you have lived your life. Based on your actions, can you say you've really lived? Can you say that you've done the best with what you were given when you entered this world from the womb?

What were we given?

Two things. First, we were given an identity. Who we are. Male or female. Whatever we become in life will be based on who we are, and that part of it will never change.

In other words, she says, you were born as Mr. Fabel, and no matter what else you may accomplish in your life-time, no matter what else you are—you are, let's say, a father, you are a writer, you are a scoundrel, but you are still Mr. Fabel. And regardless of how much the others may change, or how much one's definition of who Mr. Fabel is may change, the fact that you are Mr. Fabel will never change.

Something like that.

Yes, I think I see. But you said we were given two things. Identity is one, but what is the other?

Time. We were given an entire lifetime. We don't know how long that might be, other than that we hurdle toward death at the rate of sixty seconds per minute, so we don't try to define it any further than that.

He relates the story of the man and the mule, of shouting Hallelujah and Praise the Lawd, and he goes on to say, Yes, we should Praise the Lawd when we are led to the brink, the edge, the precipice. It is only then that we will have the courage and take the chance and walk over the edge not knowing what may happen next. He can't remem-ber where he has first heard this story, but he thinks it must have been from a friend.

Some people say there are no guarantees in life, he continues, but we're all guaranteed one thing, and that is that we will live a lifetime, however long that lifetime may be. What we do with that time is our own business, but we will use our identities to do it, and in turn it will define our identities. At the end of it we're called to account for it, for how we've used it, what we've done with it. That's what the question should be, because that is what the question is.

You make it sound as if this is the end, she says.

Isn't that what you're telling me?

I'm afraid I don't know what you're talking about.

Isn't that what this is all about? You've brought me here to defend my life, and I've already told you as much that I can't do that. I'm throwing myself on the mercy of the court. And this is where it all ends, when the lights go off altogether and the curtain falls and it's all over.

Oh no, Mr. Fabel. This isn't the end. It's just the be-ginning.

There is a moment of silence, and then Winter is stunned to hear applause coming from out of the darkness. The lights go up, and as his eyes blink in adjustment to the sudden brightness he finds that he has been talking not to a lone inquisitor sitting across a small table from him, but to an entire room full of people. Furthermore, his interrogation has occurred not in a small interview room, as he thought, nor even in an auditorium full of people, but in a television studio, complete with cameras and cameramen. And just to the left of the center camera, walking toward him, is his inquisitor: Samantha, with a big smile on her face.

Under the best of circumstances an experience of this kind might be considered too much, but Winter has come through this shock on the heels of a trip halfway across the country, after having spending the better part of the previous two days doing things he had never before imagined. It is fair to say that he has been shaken by the entire chain of events, beginning with the delivery of the airline ticket–this morning? He looks at his watch, and finds that even accounting for the time difference, it has been less than twenty-four hours since the rapping of the messenger's knuckles on his–Fabel's–door.

There is one thing that he knows for sure, however, and that is that he feels violated. He has been challenged, mocked, treated in many ways as if he were little more than a common criminal. The fact that these accusations were leveled not at him but at Fabel is not important, for Fabel is not here to answer them, but has left Winter holding the bag.

Anger wells up inside him once again. This time, however, it is directed not at Fabel (although, God knows, he has reason enough) but at Samantha. Who the hell does she think she is? And what gives her the right to ask such questions of him, or of anyone else for that matter? He has come here in good faith, willing to do what is asked of him without objection, coming straight to the studio with no idea of what is to follow, and without even a chance to unpack (being quite accommodating, he thinks, despite the unreasonableness of her request), and this is the thanks he gets for it.

Now, drenched in perspiration, his head spinning from a combination of indignation and fatigue, he fears he may pass out. He rises carefully as Samantha approaches, supporting himself by pushing against the arms of the chair in which he has been sitting, but before he knows it, before he has even had a chance to ask her what this is all about, she has slipped her arm in his like a lover or a police guard and is leading him off the set.

Congratulations, she says. That was terrific. You were terrific.

Was I? he replies coldly.

She seems not to notice, however, so flushed with excitement is she from how things have gone, and before he has a chance to say anything more she is already talking again. We have so many things to talk about, she says, I feel as if we've barely scratched the surface.

Those scratches drew blood, Winter says acidly, but she takes this as a joke and laughs.

Don't be so modest, she replies. You were even better than I expected, and my expectations were pretty high.

Her praise serves to blunt Winter's anger, even if only slightly, but it does nothing to clarify things for him. All along, he felt as if he had been on trial, but her words seem to suggest that it was actually some kind of test, a test he has apparently passed.

We'll talk about it more on the way over, she says, then stops herself. I'm sorry, she says, you must be hungry.

I ate on the plane, he replies.

Still, she says, that's no substitute, and he is forced to concede she is probably right. We'll stop first and get something.

Where are you taking me? he wants to cry out. Instead, he asks here, Where are we going?

I'm having a few people over for a reception. In your honor, of course. I imagine after this, people will want to know more about you. I know I do.

For a moment Winter's unease flares up, especially with her suggestion that there will be questions at this reception. And then he says to himself, What the hell, so be it, with a sense of fatality that has been growing steadily within him, I've come too far to turn back now. If they want me, they'll get me one way or the other. He thinks this without even an idea as to who They might be.

He looks again at Samantha as they head for the parking lot, where Ross is once more waiting for them, searching for any kind of clue that he is walking into a trap. It is the first time he has had a chance to really look at her, and he is forced to admit that the flush of excitement in her cheeks makes her quite attractive, a fact he had not noticed earlier.

In the car she thanks him once again for his appearance. You took the conversation in a completely different direction than I'd anticipated, she says. You really opened my eyes, and it isn't often that my own eyes are opened like that. Your reputation is well-founded.

And just what is my reputation, Winter asks, teasingly.

That you're truthful. And mysterious.

After a brief stop at a corner deli where he picks up a ham on rye with extra mustard, the car pulls up in front of a building located on a bluff with a view overlooking the city. Samantha's apartment is on the third floor, and there is already a crowd filling the living room when she and Winter come through the front door. Immediately, people begin to crowd around Winter, congratulating him on the appearance, and asking him questions about what he has said.

A girl who looks to be in her early twenties tells him it was the most profound thing she has ever heard. Especially when you were talking about the courage to lay down one's life for his fellow man, she says.

No, says a man dressed in a suit with an ascot tucked into his open shirt collar, I think it was when you spoke on the relationship between truth and beauty, and how true wisdom can only be found within the aesthetic of honesty.

Winter hears a woman's high-pitched laugh somewhere in the room. Music has started, a pulsing rhythm that resonates in his feet. Samantha has disappeared from his side, presumably to greet other guests. The voices in the room have grown loud, and he has to lean forward to hear someone tell him that until she heard him say it, she thought the saying Laughter is the Best Medicine was just something one read in magazines.

Yet again Winter is confused, for he has no memory of having said any of these things. Not only that, based on some of the other comments he hears, it appears that no

two people even heard the same thing. It is, he thinks, almost as if they're speaking a foreign language, one in which
he can understand their words but cannot comprehend their
meaning.

The room is not small, but neither is it large enough
for the number of people crammed in there, and as the heat
and the noise rise Winter finds himself feeling increasingly
trapped. Most of the people have drinks in their hand, and
many have joints, and as the smoke rises to the top of the
room, a sweet, sickly smell, Winter wonders if it is the combination of the two that is causing everyone to speak in such
riddles. Or perhaps, he thinks, it is having an effect on him,
creating hallucinations, and that everyone else is normal
while he is the one having the problem. Someone offers him
a gin and tonic and he accepts, glad to have something in his
hands.

Excusing himself, he manages to slip away from a
knot of people and walks through a sliding door and out
onto a balcony that overlooks the bluff and the city below.
With the door shut behind him, he is able to block out the
rising noise and the pounding music and the wafting smoke
and the chattering voices, and he hopes that the cool
nighttime air will help clear his head. He sips his drink and
watches a plane passing overhead, its wing lights winking
against the blackness of the sky and the twinkle of the stars.
It has been a long time since he has been able to see the
stars at night, such is the glare of lights in the city, and he
remembers what it was like growing up, lying on a hill on

summer nights when he didn't have to get up early for school the next day and he was able to look at the Big Dipper and the North Star and the other constellations he had read about in science books.

He takes a final swallow of his drink and, hoping it has given him some fortification, decides it would be rude of him not to return to the party, especially when he has been told it is being held in his honor. He turns and opens the door to face the crowd but finds the room is deserted, and he is all alone. Stepping aside, putting one foot carefully in front of the other, he finds it is not quite completely empty, that there is one other person in the room with him.

Alone at last, Samantha says, falling into a chair, but there is more relief than seduction in her words. Entertaining is great, but sometimes it can be such a hassle. She has changed from what she was wearing into a more casual outfit: Something More Comfortable, if you prefer the movie vernacular.

I'm sorry you went to all this trouble just for me, Winter says.

She shrugs. People were expecting it, she says. No big deal. Besides, after the high from the show, I wouldn't have been able to unwind right away.

Speaking of highs—he starts, and she laughs. I know, some people have no manners. She gets up to open the windows and air out the room.

Tell me, he asks, just what do you do?

You mean besides my work?

That, too, he says.

I'm a searcher, she replies.

Searching for what?

Whatever it is that needs finding. Sometimes it's the truth. Sometimes it's a set of missing keys.

And you said I had a reputation for being mysterious.

Naturally, she replies. Why do you think I found you so interesting in the first place?

I don't know. You tell me.

I already did once. Remember?

Humor me. It's been a long day.

Of course, she says, I'm sorry. You must be exhausted. It's late already, and with the time difference, it must be way past your bedtime.

You make me sound like a child, he says with the first outright smile he's had in several hours. Or an old man.

Only in wisdom, she replies. Why don't you stay here tonight? I can have Ross drive you back to your hotel tomorrow. It's been a long day for him, too.

Won't that be inconvenient?

It's no trouble, believe me, No trouble at all.

Thanks, he says. I'm sure your guest room beats the hotel anyway.

I don't have a guest room, she says with a shake of her head and a look that is all innocence.

Well, I don't mind sleeping on the couch, he says, warming to the banter. After today, I probably won't even notice it.

You're not sleeping on the couch, she replies.

I'm not letting you sleep there, he says.

Don't worry, I won't, she replies with a smile and a tilt of her head, the warm chestnut hair dancing across her shoulders and back.

She stands up and comes toward him, and even before it happens he knows what it will be because he has already seen the story play out many times before. She is close enough for him to smell the scent of her perfume and feel the heat from her body, and he takes hold of her arms and kisses her savagely on the lips and feels her tongue enter his mouth.

CHAPTER 20

*H*e awakens in a darkened room. At first he thinks it must be the middle of the night but a glance at the clock tells him that it is actually evening of the next day. It would not surprise him if he had slept through the entire day, but there is a tray on the table next to him with the remains of a mostly finished meal, and a newspaper lying at his feet opened to the sports section. He reaches over to turn on a lamp and, noticing a mirror over the dresser, sees that he has already showered, shaved and dressed, the bed made, and his suitcase brought over from the hotel. He then finds a handwritten note sitting next to the lamp: Will see you tonight. S.

He had apparently fallen asleep with the television on as well, for now he has identified it as the source of the noise coming at him from the far end of the room. It is tuned to an episode of an old TV series called The Man Who Never Was, with Robert Lansing playing a man named Peter Murphy, an American spy trapped in East Berlin, trying desperately to escape from Communist agents. While on the run, Murphy ducks into a bar and runs into his exact look-alike, a rich playboy named Mark Wainwright. The agents, seeing Wainwright in the bar and thinking he is Murphy, kill him, leaving Murphy free to assume Wainwright's identity—and, since the agents think they have disposed of him, free to resume his dangerous spying activities under his new cover.

Wainwright's wife Eva, played by the lovely Dana Wynter—who Winter realizes has the same last name as his own, only spelled differently; what a difference that one letter can make, he thinks—can see through the subterfuge of course, but she agrees to help Murphy with the ruse in order to keep the family fortune out of the hands of Wainwright's evil half-brother Roger. She even tells Murphy she has fallen in love with him—but has she? In an ordinary world the answer would be obvious, but East Berlin in the middle of the Cold War is anything but an ordinary world, and Murphy, a man whose very life depends on secrecy, cannot afford to be sure. Eva could be on the up-and-up, or it could all be part of a trap.

Before Winter can take this all in, the phone rings. It is Samantha, calling to let him know that she will be late, but that she hasn't forgotten about dinner tonight. Winter hadn't remembered anything at all about dinner commitments, but with this news he finds he has actually been looking forward to seeing her again and spending more time with her.

With a little time now on his hands, Winter goes to retrieve his green-covered notebook, but finds nothing there. He must have left it in his apartment in the rush to get to the airport. For the moment he is disappointed–already memories are starting to fade, and without a place to record them he is concerned some of them may disappear forever, although he wonders how he could possibly describe the remarkable events of the last few days anyway. He looks around and wanders through the apartment before finding a stack of foolscap on top of a small desk located near the front door. Also on the desktop is a calendar book, still open to yesterday's date. There is one word written in it, in the same handwriting as the note he found on the table next to the bed: Fabel.

He returns to the chair where he was sitting and begins writing. He doesn't get very far before he is interrupted by Samantha's voice. Dinner's ready, she says.

He looks up and sees her standing in the doorway to the kitchen, with the small dining room table set for two. He looks down and finds he has filled several pages with his small, cramped handrwriting.

How long have you been here? he asks. I didn't even hear you come in.

A while. You looked so intense with what you were doing, I decided not to interrupt your train of thought–you never know when a genius might be at work, right?

For some reason he has assumed they would be going out for dinner, but apparently she has prepared the meal herself. He stands up from where he has been working and walks to the table, which has a simple white cloth draped over it, and place settings for a salad, entrée and dessert. There is a pot of coffee available, and also a bottle of wine. A small vase of flowers is in the center of the table, along with two lit candles.

While they are eating the Caesar salad, they agree that after last night a little informality is in order. Call me Sam, Samantha tells Winter. You can call me—Winter hesitates for the briefest of moments—Sandy.

The room is filled with the sound of their utensils clattering on the plates, and by the time they reach the pasta tossed in herbs and olive oil, the situation calls for some kind of small talk. He recalls there was something he asked her last night, but now he can't remember what it was. So he falls back on one of the lamest questions in the book, hoping that it will appear to her as self-deprecating, rather than an act of desperation. How, he asks, did a nice girl like you wind up in a place like this?

He senses a momentary reaction of relief from her, as if she too had been looking for a way to break the silence. I suppose I could say I came West just like everyone else looking to find themselves, she replies, but I'm actually one of those rare types who was born here.

A native?

Exactly. It's given me a ringside seat to the greatest

show on earth. I've been doing this for more years than I thought I ever could, and in that time I've seen more than one person come and go, thinking their dreams were about to be answered before seeing them dashed against the rocks instead. Maybe my dream hasn't come true yet, but at least I didn't have to cross the country to look for it.

What is your dream?

I don't know, she says after a beat and a tilt of the head, similar to last night. Maybe I'm living it right now and I just don't realize it. I'm in the dream, but I can't appreciate it because I keep telling myself I'm still awake. It's only when I'm asleep that I can understand it, but as soon as I wake up it leaves me like all the dreams do. I have a vague appreciation of it, but nothing more. Maybe it means I should just stay asleep, it's a way of telling me not to try and control it all myself.

So does that mean all this–you, me, dinner–that it's all happening while you're asleep, or awake? Is it the dream or the reality? And if it's only your reality, where does that leave me? Did you just invent me? As he says this, he wonders to himself if that is what Fabel really is, just a figment of some woman's imagination?

What is reality? Sam says. Is any of this real? she adds, gesturing around the room. Not that there's anything wrong with this. I've worked hard to get where I am and achieve what I've achieved, and this is a symbol of it. I'm not dismissing it out of hand. But I think I'd go mad if you told me I had to stay here for the rest of my life. You have to take time to stop and smell the roses, but it's pretty hard to do when you're driving with the pedal to the floor all the time. Who's to say then what's real and what isn't?

She stops. But then you know about this better than I do.

What do you mean? he replies.

You know, she says. It's everything you've talked about all this time. It's one of the things that make you so interesting. One of the many things.

Finally, over a lemon custard dessert, he decides to deal with the elephant in the room. About last night–he begins.

She looks down at her plate, demurely but with the corners of her mouth slightly upturned. Well, that wasn't like me, she says shortly. I don't usually jump into something that quickly.

You weren't exactly alone, as I recall.

She smiles, and there is a twinkle in the eye. It's a lot more fun when you have a partner in crime.

Now it is his turn to smile. Nothing illegal going on, he says. Two consenting adults. No crime there.

But I wanted you to know, she says after a moment. Not to think I do that all the time.

I don't either. Sometimes these things just happen.

And I'm not sorry about it.

Neither am I.

There's something else, she says. I want it to happen again.

He pauses, then answers her: I do too.

And with that, dinner is over.

It quickly becomes a contest, her bed the playing field. They parry and feint and thrust, now attacking, now repelling, first one having the advantage, then the other. Among Sam's many pleasurable attributes, her breasts turn out to be much larger than they look when she's fully dressed, something that had escaped Winter's notice last night. (He must have been tired!) As he comes inside her, he can feel her biting at his shoulder, saying his name over and over and over. Actually, of course, she is saying the name Sandy over and over and over.

Much later, he lies awake in the honest darkness of the night. Sam has rolled over as she sleeps, lying on her side. In the meantime, Winter lies on his back, eyes wide open, hands behind his head, studying the blades of the ceiling fan as they whirl around and around. And as he does so the revelation comes to him that Sam is falling in love–not with him as she may think (for it has all been a lie on his part), but with Fabel.

No, that's not it either: she thinks that it is Fabel she loves, but in reality it is, it has to be, Winter's portrayal of Fabel. And how could Fabel possibly have been as smooth, as charming, as insightful as Winter has been while impersonating him? Any man who could travel through life leaving as little a mark as did Fabel couldn't possibly have made the kind of impression on her that Winter has. For a moment he considers the dual meaning of the words–leaving an impression, while doing an impression of Fabel. But his anger towards Fabel flares up again, this time as an irrational hatred. Forget his earlier thought of becoming friends; he is now determined to kill Fabel if he ever finds him, not just for having lived a life without merit, but for having given up on it, deserted it, and at the same time making it impossible for Winter to ever truly live in that life.

He'd have to tell her all about it, of course, explaining that he was not only a liar but a fraud as well. It was probably better to wait until morning before telling her, but another part of him wanted to get it done with right away, because he didn't think he'd be able to sleep a wink with it hanging over him. Looking at the clock glowing on the nightstand, he sees he will still have about four or five hours to wait. But looking at her lying with her bare back to him, studying the vertebrae of her spine, her left breast only partly covered by the sheet they lay under, watching her body rise and fall in steady, contented rhythms of breathing, he realizes he doesn't have the heart to wake her just yet, and allows his head to slump back on the pillow.

It is only for an instant that Winter rests his head on the pillow, but in that instant everything is shown clearly to him. He sees the face of a man much like himself, and as he studies the man's face looking for some sign of his identity, he becomes aware of a rushing sound like that of a thousand storms flying past him, and the man's body becomes enveloped in swirls of indistinct colors. The face is never obscured, but neither does it become clear. In that instant there is conception and the womb, birth and death, marriage and children and a house in the country surrounded by a low stone fence, wedding bouquets and tombstones and the eternal silence of death. There is Pete in Mexico and Ronald praising the Lawd and Collins and Driscoll and the others, and the return airline ticket sitting unused in his suitcase, and Winter all alone and lost as always; then there is only the face, and then nothing at all.

He feels something tickling his face, a gnat he thinks, or the point of a feather, and as he flicks his hand to shoo it away a shiver—more like a spasm, really—passes through his body, leaving him limp, a wet rag, as if relaxing after great stress, and in that moment the past collapses, and every second the present becomes little more than a memory. There is only the future.

And this is when it begins.

CHAPTER 21

I *t was mid-afternoon when my flight landed.*
Since I had only the carry-on, I was able to bypass the lines in baggage and head straight for the rental counter where, the email confirmation assured me, a silver Ford Mustang was waiting for me. A bit of an extravagance, perhaps, but I felt I'd earned it.

It was a busy place, even at this time of the day, and those of us here were appropriately busy people, each with our own important business to conduct. We sat at gates waiting to board our planes, walked down corridors to and from our flights, lounged in cafes and bars, with someone or by ourselves, eyes glued to the identical video screens that were everywhere in the terminal, just as they were in the stores and the storefronts and every other public place, watching but not really seeing.

We walked past advertisements that could have been from any one of a thousand cities throughout the country, with only the names changed to protect the innocent. We shared the airport as we'd shared the plane, all of us together and all of us alone, each with our own specific destinations. People working on laptops, listening to the buds in their ears, chatting on their cell phones, tweeting their friends, sharing the details of their own lives in a space full of people, with no one around to hear it. It's the way we choose to define ourselves nowadays. Who says you can't have personal space in a room full of people?

As promised, the Mustang was there when I arrived, no muss, no fuss; thanks to being a preferred member, I wasn't even required to talk with a real person to arrange it. I entered the address into the GPS, and once I made it out of the airport maze I was out on the open road. It was perhaps the first real day of summer; the sky was a clear blue with only the traces of wispy white clouds high in the atmosphere. The air was warm and gentle, without the humidity that would join up in a couple of weeks. There was a cleanliness to the whole thing, a freshness that made you glad you were in your skin.

I was content to be alone–with my thoughts, with the Mustang, with the sound of the wind as I roared down the highway. And the mechanized GPS voice, telling me to turn right, change lanes ahead, stop for gas, detour upcoming. Often when I was on a long trip I found myself giving the disembodied voice a name, and if I got bored I'd ask her questions–easy ones I knew she could answer.

Driving down the two-lane strip of road, I thought to myself: Cynthia. This is definitely a Cynthia.

Where to now, Cynthia?

Prepare to turn left.

Eventually, Cynthia informed me I'd arrived at my destination. The house was off the beaten path, about a quarter mile from the main road. A mailbox sat on a post at the edge of the pavement, and a low stone wall allowed the road to retain its definition.

As I drove along the path leading to the front door, the gravel crunched beneath the tires, and reminded me of my days as a youth at summer camp. The way was lined by trees at first, but by the time I arrived at the house they had thinned off, tall wispy blades of grass having replaced the trunks, bending hesitantly in the afternoon breeze. I could see trees behind the house and to either side, and I wondered how far back the property line went.

There was nothing prepossessing about the house, a modest affair that nevertheless bespoke a certain level of success in life. It had clean white siding against which a deep burgundy front door was set, and green shutters framed bay windows flanking the door on either side. There was a garage to the left, with the door open and a car parked outside, but not inside. It was a nice setting, I thought, a place I wouldn't mind spending some quality time myself.

I got out of the car, checking to make sure I had everything, and walked up to the door, hearing the same crunching sound under my feet. I pressed against the door-bell, heard faintly the chimes behind the door, listened to a bird crying somewhere in the distance. In a brief moment the door pulled open and I was greeted by a man's face.

In the split second before either of us spoke I was able to take in the details of that face. There were lines about the eyes and mouth and a slightly weathered texture to the skin that suggested many years spent outside, in the sun. The face was wrapped in a salt-and-pepper beard that ran down both sides of a thin, angular face. There was a minor redness along the neck where a cotton Oxford collar met the skin, an irritation that had perhaps come from that morning's shave. The hair on the top of his head had the same salt-and-pepper complexion as that on his face, thinning somewhat on top but a healthy head of hair nonetheless for a man of any age. It was combed lazily, with no particular attempt at styling, and the effect was totally in keeping with the relaxed nature of the wooded setting.

All of this I noticed in an instant, but it was the sharpness of his blue eyes that held me, and I wondered how many of my features he had been able to dissect in the same amount of time. He looked at me with the expression of one who is expecting company but nonetheless is uncertain as to whether or not the current visitor is the one he is expecting.

Mr. Fabel? I asked.

Come in, Mr. Janssen, he said, holding the door open for me as I crossed the threshold. I've been waiting for you.

I hope your flight was properly uneventful.

Worst part was going through security, I said. I appreciate you taking the time to see me.

Well, he said, shutting the door behind me, as I told you on the phone, I'm not sure how I can help. But since you'd come all this way, I figured it was the least I could do.

As he said this he gestured toward an unseen space beyond the hallway. I followed his lead and we walked into a comfortable room dominated by bookshelves (one of which had several different books with Fabel's name on the spine), a desk and a large window. I thought we'd be more comfortable here in the study, he said.

He motioned me to one of a pair of comfortable leather chairs that sat midway between the door and the desk, on the left side of the room, in front of a fireplace that lay silent at the bequest of the season. He asked if he could fix me a drink–I told him a scotch would be fine, and he walked to a small bar mounted in one of the bookcases and poured one for me, another for himself. While he poured I took a moment to assess the room. The window overlooked a garden at the back of the house. The desk, with a computer and printer sitting on its surface, faced the window, giving whoever worked there an unimpeded view of the garden. The burgundy leather of the chairs had a soft, enveloping touch to it, and I could see how someone might be quite happy working in this room, in this house, in this setting, in this life.

He returned with the glasses and settled into the chair

opposite me. I mentioned the flowers I'd seen on the walk-way up to the front door. Ranunculus, I said. Persian butter-cup.

That's very impressive, he said.

I had a case once that required me to become an ex-pert on certain types of plants and flowers, I replied. For three months I studied every day at the library, reading books written by the experts, looking at pictures. I went to flower shows, talked with the people who grew them, even passed myself off a couple of times as an expert. After that I figured I was ready, and I sprung my trap. Caught him red-handed.

I didn't imagine the private detective business was like that, he said. I pictured it as all glamour and girls, guns and action, trench coats and Bogie and Bacall.

Not likely, I laughed. If it was, I wouldn't be in the business anymore. I'd have taken a bullet to the brain a long time ago, or some dame would have gotten her hooks into me. That's not to say the job doesn't have its exciting mo-ments, but after it's all said and done it's a job just like any other. Some days are more interesting than others, but most of them are like today—a lot of travel for a few questions, follow up on some leads, try to fill in the blanks and figure out what comes next. There are times when it's more like being an accountant than anything else.

You make it sound as if it's no better than the regular 9-to-5 job.

You have to be willing to take the bad with the good,

I allowed. The job has its days, when you're confronted with an angry waitress caught borrowing from the till, or a guy wearing a wifebeater who's fallen behind in his payments and wants to take it out on you. But then there's the time when you bring a difficult situation to resolution, or solve a puzzle that has stumped everyone else, or reunite a long-lost child with her mother. Those are the good days, and the satisfaction you get from them can carry you through a week of bad ones.

He nodded. I can see where that would make up for a lot.

It does. Sometimes it doesn't seem like it's enough to make it all worthwhile. But that's only when it's been a while between good days. And besides, I wouldn't keep at it if I didn't enjoy what I do. Life's too short for that.

We talked about our work for a few minutes more, and then I got down to business. I had a feeling he was making small talk just so I wouldn't feel I'd come all the way out here for nothing, that this would somehow at least make it, as I'd said, worth my while.

I reached into a small leather bag I'd brought with me, and withdrew an envelope and from it a 3x5 snapshot. I leaned toward him and passed the photograph over, asking him if he would please take a look at it, which he did. As he studied the picture, I studied his face again. I'd memorized every feature of that photograph, looked it over a hundred times if not a thousand, and I'd gotten to the point where I could tell which aspect of it he was looking at just by the movement of his eyes.

He gave it a fair reading, neither pouring over it with the determination of a military general studying his maps nor dismissing it with the merest of glances.

Should I recognize him? he finally asked.

It depends, I said. Do you?

I can't say that I do. But obviously your presence here suggests that I should. Or at least that you think I should.

I shook my head. It would be more accurate to say that I thought you might. Or hoped you would.

Do you mind if I ask what all this is about, and what it has to do with me? You were somewhat vague about it when we talked on the phone. Since then I've welcomed you into my home and given you my booze, so I think that gives me the right to ask.

This last he said with a flicker of a smile at the corners of his mouth that took the edge off of the words.

I would have been more surprised if you hadn't asked, I replied. I then told him the story of Winter, a missing persons case I'd been hired to work on. Winter had disappeared some years ago without a trace. He'd called in sick to work one day, something he hardly ever did, and then it was as if he'd simply vanished into thin air, never bothering to come back or even call, a no-show well after he'd have been expected to recover from any serious illness. It wasn't like him, everyone had agreed, so they had feared the worst. The police had been called, the door to his apartment had been broken down, but there was no sign of him, no indication of foul play of any sort. Hospitals were called, leads were followed, but it was no use. For all intents and purposes, he might as well have passed from the face of the earth—poof. All that remained was his car, parked outside his apartment building, apparently abandoned.

You say there was no trace of him?

Not a one, I said.

The car was checked for fingerprints, I assume.

Of course. None but his own.

And there was never any evidence that he'd met with—well, you know?

Nothing that was evident. The police went through the car, his apartment, his cubicle at work. If anything had happened, whoever it was would have to have been a magician to remove the traces that thoroughly. There was nothing out of place, no sign he'd done anything illegal either at the office or in his private life. His friends couldn't recall any trouble he was in, anything he'd said that indicated he was worried about something or preparing to take a trip. The only thing to go on was that he'd withdrawn all his money from the bank the day after he'd called in sick. It was, I explained, why I felt Winter was still alive, still out there somewhere.

It was Fabel's turn now to shake his head. It's a remarkable story, what you've told me, he said, a real puzzler. But I'm afraid I still don't understand what it has to do with me, and what it was that brought you all this way. Why did you think I might recognize him, or hope that I did?

That's the interesting part of it, I said. Winter was apparently a writer himself, or trying to be one, and we ran across a few stories he'd been working on. Some of them were pretty good, actually, made me curious to read more and see where he was headed. Anyway, and this is where it really gets interesting, in this notebook along with the stories we also found your name. Several times, in fact. And while your name isn't particularly rare, you'd have to admit it isn't all that common either.

I passed a photocopy of one of the pages to him, one where his name had been written. Do you have any explanation for this?

None whatsoever, he said, handing the photograph back to me.

That's what I figured, I said. I thought perhaps he might have written to you, that he was a student or one of your readers or someone looking for advice or maybe just someone who wanted you to look at his work.

He continued to shake his head, puzzled. It's true that words can be windows to the soul, and there are people who read some that you've written and then think they somehow know you well enough to presume on you. So they do write to me from time to time. Was this man Winter one of them? Not that I can recall. Did you find any of my books in his apartment?

None that I saw. I suppose he could have borrowed them.

If you're talking about names, you'd have to admit

that his is about as common as they come. Even if I'd seen or heard his name at some point, I'm not sure I'd have remembered it. I can tell you that the face in the picture means nothing to me.

Well, thanks for trying. I figured it was a long shot at best, but something I had to check out. One last stab at finding out the truth, as it were.

You're mixing your metaphors, he said. First a shot, then a stab.

What? Oh, I see what you mean. I hadn't even noticed.

Forgive me. It was rude to interrupt you like that, but I just couldn't resist.

I slipped the picture and photocopy back inside the envelope, and the envelope back inside the leather bag.

So an abandoned car and a name found in a notebook led you all the way out here? he asked.

That's about the size of it.

I'm sorry you had to come all this way for nothing.

It's all part of the job, I told him with a shrug. The good with the bad, as I said, and you wind up going down a lot of dead ends that way, but you can't afford to take the chance that they're all that way. Sometimes, what you might think of as a dead end could be exactly what I was looking for. And besides, I added, it doesn't hurt to have an all-expenses-paid trip to a beautiful area like this, driving around in a Mustang convertible, even if it's only for a little while.

As we talked I heard a key being inserted in the lock of the door I'd come through three-quarters of an hour ago, followed by the jingle of a key chain and the rustle of bags: the lady of the house, back from the grocery store. She stuck her head in the doorway to let her husband know of her return, then saw me sitting there and quickly apologized for having interrupted us.

He motioned for her to come back into the room. There's someone I want you to meet, he said. He made the introductions, and as I stood and took her hand my impression was of a striking woman, her warm chestnut hair swirling about her shoulders, who might just be entering middle age but wouldn't have to worry about it for a few more years.

Mr. Janssen came a long way to see me, and I'm afraid I wasn't any help to him at all. The least we can do is feed him, don't you think, Sam?

Of course, she said. You'll join us for dinner, won't you? It won't be any trouble at all.

Thank you, I said. You're very kind, and I'm sure it would be delightful. But I think I'd better be going now. My work here is finished, and if I get a break with the traffic I'll just be able to get to the airport in time to catch the last flight out tonight.

With that I made my farewells, picked up my leather bag, and prepared to leave.

We walked to the door and shook hands a final time.

Tell me, he asked as I turned to leave. This Winter—do

you think you'll ever find him?

I doubt it, I said. Not if he doesn't want to be found.

CHAPTER 22

And that, I said, concludes my report.

You're sure it was him?

Of course I'm sure. It was him all right.

And the picture and the story–you say they meant nothing to him? No reaction at all?

Let me put it this way, I said. If he was lying, it was the most convincing acting job I've ever seen. And I've seen enough to know.

Remarkable, he said with a shake of his head. I must congratulate you, Mr. Janssen, on doing such a remarkable amount of work in a short time. I'm most impressed with how you were able to put it together so thoroughly.

Real life is rife with inconsistencies and loose ends, I said. Some of it is conjecture, an educated guess, a filling in of the blanks. The rest was available to anyone who wanted to look hard enough.

He nodded. And so it ends.

I watched him writing something on a legal pad with a green cover as we talked. In truth the case was difficult, one of the most difficult I'd ever worked on. I'm used to having clients hold out on me, but it doesn't mean I have to like it.

I would be paid well for the job; there were no complaints there. I got up to leave the room, my work done, but as I opened the door I turned back for a moment.

There's one thing I don't understand, though, I said.

And that is?

Why.

Why what?

Why you. Why this whole thing. Why go to the bother of it all. We all have to live within our own lives. We're born, we live and we die, and everything that happens in between is up to us. It's our job to get through it, and one way or the other we do. Does it really matter so much how we do it? A person's entitled to live happily ever after, isn't he? Even if he has to create his own life to do it?

There was no response to that—either he didn't have one or choose not to offer one. Most likely he hadn't even heard me. He had already turned away, toward something else he was studying, lost now in his own thoughts.

There was no percentage in waiting for an answer I knew I wouldn't get. My hand was still on the knob, the door still partially open, so I finished the job. I didn't even bother to look back over my shoulder as I left. Goodbye, Mr. Fabel, I said.